A FINE AND PRIVATE GRAVE

A Car'l Hobbes Mystery

Stephen Stillwell

The Vision Tree, Ltd.

This novel is a work of fiction. The author either created names, characters, locations, and events from his imagination, or used existing names, characters, locations, and events fictitiously.

Published by The Vision Tree, Ltd.
216 Waterbury Circle, Lake Villa, Il 60046
Jo@TheVisionTree.com
847.356.7550

Printed in the United States of America
ISBN: 978-1-933334-31-8

Dedication

I dedicate this book to my wonderful family:

To Zenovia, my wife of more than 50 years –
I love you more than words can say.

To my children, Annette, Michele, and Richard –
You are always in my heart.

To my grandchildren with love and laughter,
Alex, Ethan, Sean, Niki, Desaray, and LeeAnn –
I'm so proud of you all!

Acknowledgments

Many people volunteered the help and input I needed to keep my story believable. Or almost believable. There are too many to list, so I won't even try.

I'll just say thanks to all of you.

A special thank you to my daughter, Annette, for volunteering to edit this book and see it through the publishing process.

Chapter 1

"Well, Abel," Hobbes spun his wheelchair around and parked himself in back of his desk. "Did the video camera justify its expense?"

Car'l Hobbes was my boss. He had been crippled twenty years ago and worked out of a wheelchair ever since. I'm Abel Houston, his all-around handyman.

"I don't know, Chief, but it's been waiting for you. The remote is on your desk."

"Three times the witch has come," he murmured, "and fouled my front porch with the remains of a small animal that had been sacrificed. Three times, three nights, and last night became the fourth."

"Yeah, Chief," I said, "but this one we have on video."

"So we have." He pointed the remote at the large screen TV and pressed the power button. As the tube warmed up, he tossed up the remote and caught it. "Four nights ago, a dead cat was left on the step." He tossed the device again and caught it. "Next night it was a dead dog." Toss, catch. "Third was a weasel, and last was...," toss — miss. It clattered on his desk, and he snapped it up. "And last night would have been a rat." He ignored my grin. Instead, he said, "I could understand it if we lived in Roswell."

He was talking about the remote, not the animals. He virtually never missed in his game of toss and catch, and he looked at me suspiciously. He placed the remote squarely in the middle of his desk and stared at it, daring it to move. It didn't.

"And no indication yet as to who left the animals those first three nights," I said, completing his observation. Then I added, "Meridian is stranger than Roswell. Anyhow, now we have a video of whatever happened on the fourth night." I glanced at the remote. "If the playback equipment still works."

Things had a way of happening around here, like Murphy's Law had taken up residence.

"It will work, all right. Will it be a rat this time?" Hobbes didn't believe in Murphy's Law.

"I'd bet on it."

All of the animals so far represented three of the four trinals — or groups of three — that had been part of a coven of demon-worshipping self-declared witches. Those animals had been tossed on the front steps of Hobbes' old house. All of them had their heads torn off. Last night would have been the last visit, if the animals symbolized what I thought they did.

Sixty seconds passed before he picked up the remote and pressed the *play* button. The eight-foot projection TV screen came to life.

We leaned forward and watched.

The clock imprint on the videotape showed 2:00 a.m. The infrared sensor brought the camera to bear on the trespasser and followed her automatically as she scurried from the Colorado blue spruce at the corner of the house to the shelter of the privet hedge in the front. She ran bent over, stopping once when a car went by and again when she reached the bottom steps.

She wore a black cape and a black pointed hat with a floppy brim that hid her features.

We couldn't identify the woman, but she was bigger than life on Hobbes' eight-foot TV screen. Halloween-kind of scary. A witch or someone who wanted us to think she was a witch.

After a few seconds, she opened a gunny sack and took out a dead rat, its head barely attached to its body. She finished the separation and tossed it all onto the top step. She was more comical than frightening.

I didn't know what was going through Hobbes mind, but I laughed out loud.

She stepped the four steps onto the porch and leaned against the rail directly under the camera. The witch kept her face in the shadow of the floppy brim as she looked slyly toward the camera. She shook her head, stretched out her arms, and beckoned with her hands. Then, she abruptly reached inside her cape and brought out a double–edged hatchet, stepped back to throw it, and in one graceful move fell backward over the porch railing.

Less than ten seconds later, she was back on the porch with the hatchet in her hand. This time she didn't step back. For an instant the hatchet waxed large as it flew directly into the camera. The picture changed to snow.

"Too bad," I muttered. "I would like to have seen the broom she rode in on."

"An expensive camera," Hobbes added.

I shut off the TV.

"Who is she?" he asked.

"She's not the lady next door."

"No," he agreed, "not Katya Ransom. She has been staying with the Butlers for only a few weeks, Abel. She may have been a witch somewhere, but I don't think she's had enough time to settle in here."

"Yeah? Well, I suppose you're right. We could probably narrow it down to one of the members of the old coven, though, couldn't we?"

Hobbes cocked his head in thought. "Or someone who knew about it. That's a long time to hold a grudge."

"Who else could it be, Chief?"

"You have admirers, Abel, and friends who are practical jokers." He sighed. "And now that she has allowed herself to be taped, she is unlikely to return, so you may be finished with her, anyway."

"You know, Chief, it wouldn't be hard to check around and see if anyone is missing a cat or a dog."

Hobbes shrugged. "Possibly, but to what purpose? If you knew who the witch was, would you call the police?"

I shook my head, "Probably not. Tough on the animals, but what can you do?"

He waved his hand, "Not even for a damaged video camera. In the meantime, we must look to the future. Do we not have new clients coming today?"

With that, he put the witch and the stuffed animals behind us. A new case was about to open up.

"Yes sir," I said, "One fifteen. They made the appointment two weeks ago. I can tell you what I know about them in five minutes, maybe four. But, if I tell it all, there won't be any surprises."

He raised an eyebrow.

"The surprises are few. Even Sally found nothing, or next to nothing."

"Then we need not take any special precautions?"

I shook my head, "If any clients were ever harmless, then these people coming today are them."

He smiled, the corners of his mouth turning up barely an eighth of an inch. "Clients are seldom harmless."

"Wait 'til you meet them."

"Then call me at one." He spun his wheelchair around and headed toward the kitchen. I went to the small office by the front door and played e-mail catch-up on the computer.

The grandfather clock that claimed a special place in the main hallway finally showed one o'clock — without chiming. The chimes had been turned off years ago when Hobbes decided the clock was too close to his bedroom. I'd always felt it deserved better, but it was his house.

He paid the bills and our salaries, and he was the boss. So I whistled out the hour's Westminster chimes, said "bong" loud enough for him to hear, once, and let it go at that.

Hobbes, if he went according to routine, would make a face at his cup of cold instant coffee, push his paper plate to the back of the table, give Fred a curt,

"Company's coming," grab a couple of Fosters from the fridge, and then wheel out of the kitchen, down the hall and into the great room. There, he would put the beers inside the small refrigerator near his desk — for later in the day. Only then would he be ready to go to work. Sure enough, Hobbes stayed true to form.

Fred held the kitchen door for him and said, "Gotcha, Boss." A few minutes later he brought out the cart with the cups, cream and sugar, and a coffee pot filled with water and real coffee grounds. He parked it just inside the great room, but he didn't plug it in. He left that up to me.

I grabbed the old *National Echo* from the hall table and went into the great room, plugged in the coffee pot, and waited for the boss to notice me.

Fred said "Afternoon, Abel," satisfied himself that the place was ready for visitors, and went back to his kitchen — to do whatever he did back there. I was pretty sure it wasn't cooking.

I wondered briefly if the room was too cool for the guests, who were old enough that they might be sensitive to temperature. I decided to crank the thermostat up a couple of degrees, just in case.

Hobbes would not be bothered by the cost of comfort. He had his ways of saving money.

On the one hand, he drank cheap beer and kept a cook who was afraid of fire, but who worked for next to nothing. The boss claimed that premium beer was a waste of money, and if he wanted eggs benedict for breakfast, there was a Denny's close by. On the other hand, he normally kept the entire house at a cool seventy degrees, and that ten-room century-old house on River Street took a lot of cooling. I'd written out checks for the electric bill and each one confirmed my belief; the money he saved on beer in one month would not have paid for one hour of cooling.

I struck a pose near the south window while I waited. The view there was much better than the view from the front window. It overlooked the river, and for a while I enviously watched the youthful skiers who flew over the water. A quarter of a mile away, the towropes were invisible so that the skiers appeared to chase the rocket-powered boats that led them, overcoming gravity and centrifugal force as if they were gods of the river.

The gentle whisper of rubber wheels on hard carpet stopped at the desk a few feet in back of me.

"Have you read today's horoscope, Chief?" I turned, trying to keep my expression neutral as I handed him the newspaper.

"I try not to trouble myself."

"It's right here, in the *Echo*. I circled it with a red pencil."

He sighed, but took the paper anyway. A moment later, he lowered it to his lap and gazed thoughtfully at me. "Abel," he said. "I seldom read these things, but you apparently think this would interest me: 'Capricorn.'"

He studied the paper as if looking for something subtle and elusive. "'Capricorn; Prepare to deal with a peculiar situation involving twins!'"

He dropped the paper on his desk and looked at me with suspicion. "You are obviously attempting some machination, Abel. This is not even today's paper."

"Me?" I said. "Machination?" I'd had to search through a month of old newspapers to find something that would kick–start his brain before the clients started beating down the door. "A famous detective once said, 'All horoscopes are interchangeable, and if that's so, what difference does the day make?'"

He leaned back in his wheelchair and closed his eyes briefly, "I should also have said, 'A quiet stroll through the garden can be ruined by the cawing of a witless crow.'" Then he added, "Would you bring me a coffee, Abel?"

It was the way things were; his wheelchair limited him to a degree, so I brought him his coffee –– a little cream, a little sugar –– and sat it on his desk.

He returned to the paper. "Even if you are being devious, this is curious. Twins, I believe, are somewhat unusual in a horoscope, even though Gemini is the third sign of the Zodiac, and one might expect twins to get equal exposure. You would not anticipate contact with them on any particular day, would you?" He paused and then added, "How tenuous do you suppose a contact could be and still be called a contact?"

The doorbell interrupted him. He glanced at the mantel clock and nodded. The client was on time and he was ready to go to work. As for clients, he liked to meet them without having any preconceptions, so he seldom knew who would ring the doorbell.

He left it to me to set up the first meeting –– he was a believer in first impressions. Of course there were times when ignorance could be more deadly than bliss. He tried to get past the ignorance part as quickly as possible.

We heard Sally call out, "I'll get it!" A moment later, a flash of lavender passed the open door to the hallway.

"Yes, yes, please come in. Kindly wait here."

I had not seen Sally Wilson, "Cemetery Sally," as we sometimes called her — for three or four days, and she sounded incredibly cheerful. I glanced around the room and caught Hobbes' eye. He shook his head slightly and mouthed, "No cut flowers."

She entered the office a bit out of breath and danced across the floor, circling the room to pass the two couches and four of the chairs, and then paused to bow briefly at the large screen TV at the other end of the room. She stopped in front of Hobbes and bowed again, extending her right hand. Pinched between her thumb and forefinger was a business card. His face expressionless, Hobbes took the card and glanced at it briefly. "Show him in."

"Him? Him? Nay, good sir. Them!" She turned, and dashed back to the hallway. A slightly raised eyebrow told me that Hobbes wished, not for the first time, that someone else would answer the doorbell.

"This way! This way, now. He awaits!" She showed three people through the door with elaborate curtseys, but they held back until she stepped aside. Their alarm faded slowly as they paused and took stock of the room, gazing first at the shoulder-high bookcases that covered most of two walls where windows weren't in the way, and then at the two gas fireplaces.

"Sally!" Hobbes spoke sharply. "Thank you, my dear; that is enough. You may leave."

She winked at him, smiled, curtsied, did a pirouette, and with her hands pointed above her head and touching, danced on her toes from the room.

He watched with his usual inscrutability as she left, then smiled slightly and faced his guests.

Chapter 2

Two women and a man, all apparently in their mid seventies, gazed back at him.

The man spoke first. He had made the appointment, but all he could say after watching Sally leave was, "Oh, yes..." as he stared after her. Age had not treated him well: at one time, he must have been over six feet tall, but a chronic slump had robbed him of three or four inches. His hair was unnaturally dark, and his moustache gray. He wore a perpetual squint, but no glasses, and when his face had gone pale on meeting Sally, it had revealed two faint scars tracing their way down his left cheek. He was dressed well enough in a light gray suit, but I thought it was a few years out of date. Even his leather briefcase shone with the patina of age, although it didn't seem very much used.

Hobbes took a moment to study the women before saying anything. Both were of medium height and slender; both stood erect and silent. One had vivid red hair and clear blue eyes — eyes that were sharp and piercing, even through very thick lenses. Her tan suit looked expensive and custom made.

The other woman was hidden in a black dress that reached her wrists and ankles. A black veil covered her face. Her only concession to color was a light gray knit shawl. She walked to a Queen Anne chair in a distant corner of the room and sat down in a single graceful movement. Hobbes glanced at me briefly and wheeled himself around the back of his desk.

I picked up two armless upholstered chairs and placed them near the left side of the desk, offering my arm to the lady in the suit. She ignored me, walking to one of the chairs and seating herself. After a moment, the man sighed, and then slowly, as if he had all at once turned very old, took the other chair. I looked pointedly at the woman in the corner; the man shook his head. "She'll be all right," he said after a deep breath. None of them offered to shake hands, but Hobbes wasn't offended. It was a common omission in his wheelchair life.

The man studied the door that Sally had used in her enthusiastic exit. "Is she," he hesitated, "Is she...." He glanced at Hobbes, then at me, then sideways at the woman in the veil, as if he needed help deciding what question to ask.

Hobbes understood, and said, "No, she is neither crazy nor an idiot."

"She reminds me of a spiritualist I once knew."

"She is also no spiritualist." After a brief pause, he continued. "You are here on business, having made an appointment with Mr. Houston. I assume that you know my reputation, that it is my job to debunk and discredit those who claim spiritual powers or contacts — not hire them."

It always seemed odd to hear him talk that way — with his bald head, angular face and almost pointed ears. When he closed his eyes to eighth-inch slits, he might well have been from some nether region of the underworld, himself. His droopy moustache didn't do much to lessen that image. Years ago, when he was a police lieutenant and could stand, he had the look of a predator — maybe a tiger, lean and hungry — whose gaze could command caution in any adversary. Denied legs, he made do with the wheelchair and a powerful voice.

"Oh, yes. Yes, I know," said the man. "You believe all such people are frauds. You help get rid of their ghosts."

Hobbes shook his head mildly. "No, I do not get rid of ghosts. I cannot rid you of something that does not exist. That goes for everything else about the paranormal as well. In my limited experience, I have found all claims of supernatural events to be nothing more than hoax, fraud, or delusion. I have conducted hundreds of investigations and not one has successfully endured scientific inquiry."

He paused and sipped his coffee. Studying a new client was a pivotal part of all of his first meetings with a new client, and now and then, someone would get up and leave. They had mistakenly come to talk to the dead –– to be reassured that there was another side to existence –– and found that Hobbes, Inc. was the wrong place for that.

This time as he studied the trio carefully, no one seemed inclined to say goodbye, so Hobbes continued, "I always try to make it clear to potential clients that my job is to be a skeptic. In doing that job, I get paid to expose deceptions, whether they be innocent pranks, or cruel ruses crafted for gain. Keep this in mind if you wish to engage the services of this firm."

"We understand –– we all understand." The man pulled slowly at his ear, "That skepticism is exactly what brought us here."

"Then," said Hobbes, "We should start with introductions. I am Car'l –– with an apostrophe –– Hobbes. I founded this firm several years ago after an accident left me without the use of my legs. I have, however, surrogate legs in the form of my associate, Mr. Houston, whom you see leaning against my bookcase." All eyes turned toward me long enough to see a brown–eyed, dark–haired man about six feet tall with a few faded burn scars on his face and hands. I gave them my best smile and moved away from the bookcase on Hobbes' surrogate legs to lean against the wall.

"And you are," he didn't bother to glance at the business card, "Avery Regasmun, attorney for the ladies?"

"Ah, yes," Regasmun affirmed. "Their attorney. But I've also been a family friend for over sixty years, since the three of us were children. Next to me," he said without turning his head, "is Judith Borden. In the corner is her sister, Gloria. There is a brother, younger by fifteen years, whose name is Cassius. It is because of him that we are here."

He had regained his composure and flashed a broad, toothy smile that was at odds with eyes that shifted rapidly from person to person, but fit nicely with hair that was black and curly. He was trying to look sixty, and maybe at a distance, he did.

Judith put her hand on Avery's wrist and squeezed. He winced, but did not look at her. "You'll take forever, Avery," she said. "Close your mouth. I'll tell the story." Light glinted off her glasses, and her eyes were large and cold behind them.

"Have you heard of my sister, Mr. Hobbes?"

14

He nodded, "Gloria Borden, yes. As I recall, her name has been historically paired with that of Eldred Carpunky, with whom she claimed spiritual contact. They were quite famous in the late fifties. I have wondered if 'Carpunky' was a real name."

Judith Borden ignored the implied question. "You should say the ghost of Eldred Carpunky," she corrected, her tone mild. "The *ghost*. They are still famous. Read the tabloids. Read the *National Echo,* Mr. Hobbes. A reporter attended a sitting two months ago. Read what he said."

"I did," he responded dryly. "A most favorable report."

"He was not a fool, Mr. Hobbes."

"I know of him, Miss Borden, and you're right; he's not a fool." She frowned, as if she suspected Hobbes was mocking her, but he continued, "Perhaps it would be wise to assume that we are ignorant of all details, and for you to tell us what you want to in your own way."

"All right." She closed her eyes for a moment and let her face relax. Wrinkles faded, and a hint of the beauty she must once have been shone for an instant.

"About forty years ago," she began, "Shortly after we moved into that oversized old house –– I find it amusing that some people call it a mansion –– in the Gold Coast area of Chicago, my sister made her first contact with the dead man. I have since been told it was unusual for a woman of her age to become a spirit medium — that most begin in their early teens. Nevertheless, contact was made.

"It started in what you might call the traditional way, with a knocking during the night. It wakened Gloria first, in her bedroom. She called out to me, and I rushed to her. She had left her bed, and was sitting in the darkness in an armless chair, much like this one. She seemed about ready to fall off. I steadied her with my hands on her shoulders. The skin under her gown was like ice. 'Did you hear it?' she asked me. I shook my head. 'Hear what?' 'The knock,' she answered. I said I'd heard nothing.

"A moment passed, and I thought she must have had a bad dream. Then, I heard what she had heard: two faint sharp taps, a pause, and then a third tap. It seemed to come from the floor, but it was not the sound of someone knocking on wood. It was less substantial than that. Muffled, as if it had to travel through some barrier. Although the tapping did not seem threatening, I immediately went to Gloria's telephone and called the police.

"They searched for intruders. As I said, it is a large house. There are five bedrooms — including Gloria's — and three bathrooms on the second floor. Gloria's room was right above the library, but there was no evidence of anyone standing on something to tap on the ceiling. The police search was unsuccessful. On his way out, one of the policemen made a joke that the house must be haunted.

"Gloria went back to her room, still frightened —— still agitated. But she was excited, too, thrilled by the prospect of something that was new, perhaps even dangerous. She refused my offer to call a doctor and returned to the chair. She asked me to turn the lights off and I waited with her — in darkness broken only by the moonlight coming through the window. After a while, the three taps with the pause came again.

""Who is there?' I called out, but there was no answer. 'Speak to us!' I demanded. Still there was no response.

"Then Gloria whispered, 'Who..., who is there?'

"The same three taps were repeated.

"'Will you talk to me?' Two quick taps.

"'Are you going to hurt me?' One tap.

"'Who are you?' Tap, tap, pause, tap.

"She looked at me, puzzled, but I knew we were both thinking the same thing. Whatever it was, ghost or spirit or demon, the policeman had unwittingly spoken the truth –– the house was haunted, and whatever it was, it was trying to communicate with Gloria. When I look back on that night, Mr. Hobbes, I still find it strange that neither of us was afraid. Do you think we should have been frightened?"

Hobbes shrugged, "I have no way of looking into the past, nor do I have recourse to supernatural help. You say you were alarmed, but not frightened. I find that remarkable in itself."

In the corner of the room, from the woman in the black veil, came a short, sad, gentle cry. Icy fingers moved up my back. "Gloria!" Judith's voice was sharp and commanding. The cry stopped.

"The house was haunted," she repeated, "and its ghost wanted to communicate with us. It found a way to do so by knocking. It didn't take long for us to realize that two knocks meant 'yes', one meant 'no', and three knocks meant it couldn't answer the question. It also became obvious that it would respond only to Gloria. For the next ten minutes or so, she questioned it:

"'Are you a man or a woman?' Tap, tap, pause, tap. Bad question — no 'yes' or 'no' answer.

"'Are you a man?' Two taps; yes.

"'Were you murdered?'

"Ghosts, we had heard, were likely to have been victims of foul play, and were stuck here, incomplete, waiting for... justice, maybe.

"Two taps; yes.

"'Do you know who killed you?'

"For a moment there was no answer, then suddenly, Gloria cried out, 'Judith, take my hands.' When I did, she dropped into a trance and started talking. Her voice became deep and masculine. He was talking to me using Gloria as a channel. She was completely unaware of what he said.

"'I am Eldred' it said — he said. 'I am dead? Why am I dead?'

"'I don't know,' I answered. 'What do you want?'

"'I want justice.'

"'What can we do to bring you justice?' I asked.

"Eldred was silent for a while, then he said, 'Bring people to me. I will answer their questions until you finally bring me the one who can answer mine.'

"Then, he quit talking to us and was gone.

"The next day, a reporter rang our doorbell and very politely told us he'd heard from the police about a 'haunting,' and wondered if he could interview us. In our naiveté, we agreed, and over iced tea and lemon wafers, told him the entire story.

"We watched the daily newspapers, but there was nothing about us in any of them. We thought that perhaps the event had not been newsworthy and had simply been dropped. "But the next Friday, the story appeared on the front page of the *National Echo*."

Chapter 3

"'*Local Spinsters Talk to Ghost of Murdered Man!*' the headline read. Spinsters, indeed. We are spinsters now, sir. Then, we were in our mid-thirties. I felt insulted and badly used — made into a spectacle for prying eyes. My sister found it amusing." She paused. "Do you find us amusing, Mr. Hobbes?"

"Not at all, Miss Borden. However, this may become a long afternoon. Would you like something to refresh your throat?"

She glanced at Regasmun, and then nodded.

I circled the desk and chairs and stuck my head into the hallway. "Fred!" I called. It annoyed Hobbes that I wouldn't pull the cord that rang the bell in the kitchen. I was holding out for a push button, which I had told him he could have installed with the money he'd save on ten cases of cheap beer. He'd insisted the pull cord was cheaper. And it was already there.

A moment later, Fred tromped into the living room. 'Tromped' was the right word — he was wearing black fireman's boots.

"Fred," Hobbes said. "Would you bring some drinks for our guests?"

"Can they talk? All they got to do is tell me what they want and I'll get it for 'em. I got cheap beer, cheap wine, cheap whiskey —"

"Miss Borden?" I directed my question to Judith. Fred would have continued with his litany of cheap drinks if I hadn't stopped him. Besides, the only cheap drink in the house was the beer.

"Water would be fine," she replied.

Fred nodded.

"Gloria would like a glass of port, and Avery would take a martini, on the sweet side," she continued.

"Olive or onion?" Fred asked.

"With a sweet martini?" Miss Borden shuddered. "What difference could it make?"

"I'll have coffee," Hobbes said, and seeing the look in Fred's eyes, amended, "Iced coffee."

"Chocolate for me," I said, "*Hot* chocolate." Fred glared at me and slowly backed out of the room, his eyes never leaving mine.

"Please continue, Miss Borden." Hobbes said.

"Very well.

"On the following Monday, we received three telephone calls from spiritualists, a dozen or so from people who wanted us to contact dead relatives and two from parapsychologists who wanted to perform an examination of the house. By the end of the week, we had received over fifty calls. We took telephone numbers when we could, and promised to call back.

"On Tuesday, Eldred spoke through Gloria again. I asked him what he wanted us to do. He said he would appear at sittings — or séances, as we used to call them — as often as we wished. We could ask him whatever we wanted to about other departed people, and he would answer as he could.

"During that first real sitting, with only Gloria and me, I asked him how long he had been at our house. He said time had no meaning to him. Had he died here? He answered, 'I am dead? Why am I dead?' Those seven words became almost a trademark for Eldred, like a mantra. He asked them at the beginning of every séance, even when the demand for Gloria's services became so excessive that we began charging for them –– and we were able to charge a great deal as her reputation grew.

"Over the years, our success grew. If we had not already been wealthy, we could have become so. I will not describe a sitting for you; I expect you to take part in one. You should know in advance that there will be no moving furniture, no screaming or graphic reenactment of murder, only indisputable evidence of spirit communication." She paused, and looked at the lawyer.

"Avery will explain about our brother, Cassius."

But the clomp, clomp of rubber boots delayed Avery's explanation.

Fred returned, carrying a tray. This time, he wore insulated gloves. He came to me first and gave me my cup of hot chocolate. I was almost ashamed of myself; he looked ready to cry. He passed the rest of the drinks around and then stomped out of the room. "Flaming Saganaki for supper tonight, Fred?" I called after him.

"Our cook used to be a fireman," Hobbes said, as if that explained anything. "I believe he is preparing to cook supper. Now, please go on, Mr. Regasmun."

"Oh, yes. Yes." He seemed a little perplexed. "Well, Cassius is young, only sixty, and he has a lot of desires, among those a great need for money. And, well, Judith and Gloria have a lot of money. Their home alone would bring several million dollars if they chose to sell it. Cassius thinks he can have his sisters declared mentally incompetent because of the... because of the ghost. He could then become their legal guardian. I doubt that he has much chance for success, but there is the annoying possibility that a court would favor his request. He is a robust man, and the sisters are at an age where a young court might expect to find diminished capacities.

"Therefore we want you to investigate Judith and Gloria to prove the truth of their claims. You will have to work your way back through forty years, examine newspaper reports and interview those clients who are still available. We expect you to attend one or several sittings, to look through the house for tricks and hidden doors, wires, TV cameras — whatever you do to uncover a hoax. We want you to prove that Gloria does as she says."

Hobbes brought both hands to his moustache and gently drew his fingers down to the ends. "It is unlikely," he said slowly, "that I will prove she communicates with a dead man. I already have no doubt about her being a fraud, and that is almost certain to be the conclusion I will reach during my investigation. If I undertake what you request and later appear in court as a witness, it will be as an expert, and I will not perjure myself on your behalf. Is that clear?"

"Perfectly. We want nothing but your expertise and a complete, accurate report."

"Then I am baffled. If I cannot validate your claim, and I don't think you expect me to, what good will I be to you?"

Regasmun showed all his teeth again, "Very simple, Mr. Hobbes. If you prove that Gloria is indeed a fraud, that she has deliberately perpetrated a hoax, and is still doing so, then the incompetence charge will be irrelevant and we will have a criminal case.

"Believe me when I say I would much rather defend her in a criminal case. Cassius' assertion of incompetence would disappear."

"Remarkable," Hobbes murmured. "And what does Gloria think of this? It is, after all, her reputation, and maybe self-respect, that is at stake."

Judith answered, "She concurs; she knows it's necessary. She will —"

"*I* will!" The words came from the far corner of the room in a voice soft and intimate. "At first I did not agree with your hiring, Mr. Hobbes, but I would have allowed it. Now I am glad we came. You may help in ways not yet discussed. I think you will solve an old, old mystery."

She came around to the right side of Hobbes' desk, and looked at him through the black lace. I edged around in back of his chair and watched.

"Eighteen minutes, Mr. Hobbes," she said enigmatically, pulling the pins that secured her veil to free her hair. A cascade of brilliant red fell to her shoulders. I looked at her sister and back again. The biggest difference was in the eyes, hers were warm, friendly, almost inviting. "By eighteen minutes, I am the older sister, and because of that fact of birth order, our father's will gave me control of his estate for my lifetime. When I wish to do so, I, Gloria Borden, make the final decisions — the legal ones, not Judith or Avery. Before coming here, I had merely agreed to hire you. Now, because of things said at this meeting, I insist on it. Have I made myself clear?"

She seemed unnecessarily emphatic, and I sensed that some subtle change in the relationship among the three had just happened. However, I didn't know them well enough to guess what it was.

"Indeed you have, Miss Borden. We shall be antagonists, and my job will be to show the world that you are a fraud. We may become enemies. If you understand and accept those conditions, then I shall consider it a privilege to work for you."

"Thank you Mr. Hobbes. But I promise you that we will not become enemies. You will fail to prove I am a fraud, and we shall be friends." She smiled at Hobbes and then at me, carefully replaced her veil, and then returned to her chair in the far corner.

Hobbes looked at his desk. The *National Echo* laid where he had put it, still open to the horoscope section; "...*a peculiar situation involving twins...*" He looked at me, one eyebrow raised a sixteenth of an inch. I looked back in mock innocence. Twins. Of course I had done some basic research on the Bordens after Regasmun had made the appointment.   A guy has to have a little fun, now and then. That's how kick–starting the boss works.

Hobbes did the double hand-stroke of his moustache again, then made his hands into a tent and brought his fingers to touch his chin. "Perhaps," he said, "we should discuss fees and expenses, and of course, the retainer."

Chapter 4

Hobbes has his ancient house on River Street, with its maintenance and taxes, plus a staff of four — I haven't talked about Charon, the boat-keeper, yet — whose salaries he has to pay, and that is how he justifies his fees, which are generally exorbitant, but not always. There are some exceptions. This was not one of them.

Actually, these clients didn't even blink as they signed a contract to pay a hefty retainer now and an additional small fortune later — when the job was completed — plus expenses. For the small fortune, he would prove to a court that Gloria was a fake, if such was the result of his investigation. On the other hand, they would pay the same amount if he proved that she was the real thing; either result would be acceptable – – the catch being that if he got no positive results, then all he would get were the retainer and expenses. He would walk, or rather roll, away without the big bucks. It was a strange agreement that could take a lot of time and just possibly have no payback. My guess was they expected Hobbes to have a lot of trouble.

But, I wasn't too worried. I had been with him for over twenty years, and I figured he had at least a fifty percent chance of success. If he wasn't concerned, neither was I.

After her one brief exchange with Hobbes, Gloria said nothing more. When the contract had been signed by Judith and witnessed by Avery, I took it to her and she added her signature without bothering to read it.

Judith wanted Hobbes to come to their Chicago home and begin the investigation immediately. When told that the house had many stairs but lacked wheelchair access, he politely refused.

"If it's necessary to come later, I shall, with Abel and Fred to assist me. In the meantime, Abel — Mr. Houston — will be my eyes and ears, as well as my legs. He is fleet of foot and an excellent observer, though he, like the rest of us, has shortcomings, his being impatience and impetuousness. He will go to your home, use his wit and intuition to gather fact and fable as well as impressions, and report to me. The firm will consult and then conceive a course of action."

Judith interrupted, "When?"

"When do we begin? We have already begun." Hobbes glanced at the anniversary clock with its glass dome and rotating brass balls that sat on the mantel above the east fireplace; "It is two hours before supper. I invite you to eat with us, although I suspect it will be cold chicken and melon. Until then, I would like all of you to give us details about the people who live with you and about the physical structure and layout of your house, especially the room where you have your sittings."

Judith pursed her lips as if deciding what not to say. "Gloria and I share our house with our niece, Marilyn, and our housekeeper, Gladys. Marilyn is thirty-two and teaches at the University. She has lived with us since she was a child." Judith allowed a small measure of pride to enrich her voice, and again her features softened for a moment. Then she continued, "Gladys was with us when we moved into the house. We are a quiet, refined household, Mr. Hobbes." I glanced toward Gloria. Was it my imagination, or had she snorted? "Cassius frequently has dinner with us and often joins the sittings, as does Avery."

For the rest of the meeting, it was question and answer, with Hobbes asking, and mostly Judith answering, with Regasmun adding once that he, too, was a frequent visitor, and yes, he had power of attorney for the sisters and paid their bills. They talked a lot about the room where they had the sittings, from which I got a pretty good picture of the furniture arrangement and such, but no clear feeling about it. I decided to wait until I saw it for myself before forming an opinion. Hobbes paused now and then to stroke his moustache, and study his clients. Finally, he leaned back in his wheelchair.

"I think we have enough to consider until Abel returns from your home. Tomorrow is Saturday. He can be there in the morning."

They agreed — the sooner, the better.

They declined the offer for supper — apparently cold chicken and melon appealed to them as much as it did to me — and shortly before six, I showed them out. I wasn't surprised to see a limo waiting for them.

Gloria stopped on the top step of the front porch and studied the small flower gardens that had been planted near the house. "Lovely," she said in a dreamy voice. "Who takes care of them?"

"Charon, our boatman."

"They are beautiful. Does the River Styx pass nearby? Charon ferried the dead across it, you know, on their way to Hades."

"No, it's the River Illinois that passes nearby. Charon sometimes crosses over in the rowboat, but not to Hades, just to the plain old Meridian State Hospital, otherwise known as MerSH."

"Not to Hades?"

"Maybe to Hades, in a manner of speaking. Some MerSH residents may think of it that way."

She gave me a glowing smile and then walked down the steps and across the sidewalk to the limousine.

Before she could get in, Katya Ransom appeared from behind the blue spruce that separated our driveways, and stormed her way past Regasmun to within inches of Gloria's face. Katya's enormous cat, Harmless, followed her from behind the tree and gracefully jumped into the back seat of the limo.

"You don't belong here. Now, get out!" Katya's words seemed sharp enough to scrape the paint off the steps, had she been closer.

"My dear Katya," Gloria answered gently. "How nice to see you. How is your husband?"

"Go back to your fortune-telling," Katya hissed. "We are witches here!"

Regasmun tried to pull Harmless from the car, but stepped back when the cat bared his claws.

Gloria said, "Come, Harmless. Out. We have to leave, and you must stay." The cat jumped from the car, ran toward the Butler's house, and disappeared under the front porch.

Gloria touched Katya's hand. "You must come see us sometime my dear."

Katya whispered something that I couldn't hear, and Gloria laughed. Katya grimaced, turned around and gave me a warning glance, as if daring me to comment. Then she walked stiffly back to the Butlers', up the steps, and into the house.

Regasmun helped Gloria into the limo. Judith ignored his offer and entered unassisted. Regasmun then took a seat next to the driver. Gloria waved goodbye as they drove away.

When I came back to the living room, Hobbes had the phone book open.

"Pizza?" I asked.

He nodded.

"Salad and diet?"

He grunted, then read me the number. I dialed.

While we waited, I told him what had happened outside, and asked, "Is Katya a part of this, or is her knowing the Bordens just a coincidence?"

"Few things are coincidental," he murmured. He seemed disinclined to discuss it further.

Thirty minutes later, Hobbes, Sally and I served ourselves pizza and salad at the kitchen table while an ignored Fred ate cold chicken and melon with Charon in the boathouse.

It was a working supper in that we discussed the case, with Hobbes giving instructions for the rest of the evening and tentatively for the next day, depending on what Sally found out that evening.

Now that the firm was on a job, Sally was all business — a skilled research person. "Give me one hour on the Internet," she had once said, "and if what you want is there, I'll find it!" I didn't think she was that good, but, what the heck, she was a lot better than me.

For a lot of our needs, though, the archives of public libraries were much more rewarding. She was a familiar sight at the one in Meridian. Not that libraries were her only option. She claimed to know of countless sources in the public domain and seemed to thrive on digging deep into records at courthouses, local museums, and newspaper archives.

"I need," Hobbes told her, "information on the Borden sisters, Eldred Carpunky, the house, the haunting, whatever you think is relevant. Right now, I just want an overview. We'll go for detail later as we require it."

Sally smiled and looked at me, but she handed the thin brown envelope to him.

"Abel made the appointment two weeks ago, Chief, so I had time to do a little preliminary research, and I want you to know that *little* is the key word for the results. I spent an entire morning at the Chicago Public Library on State Street, and what I found about the Bordens is in that envelope. It's barely a start, but it does tell a little about their public image for the past forty years, including the fact that they have a lot of money."

Her smile faded. "The newspapers, especially the tabloids, sometimes make a big deal over supernatural happenings, but the only one that consistently followed the Bordens was the *National*

Echo. When I went to their office, which was also downtown, and asked if I could see their files on the Bordens, the editor-in-chief, Tom Wilder, came down to tell me to get lost."

Hobbes opened the envelope and glanced over Sally's report. "Do not feel badly about the *Echo,* Sally. We had a legal confrontation some eighteen years ago and the tabloid lost. It cost them a hundred thousand dollars and a front-page apology. Wilder has never gotten over it, but life does go on."

He turned to me. "I want you to pack for three or four days, although you may be there only half that time. Take your tool kit, recorders, UV and infrared cameras, and the other tools of our trade, but don't expect too much from them. Those people are well prepared for you, having been the object of scrutiny for four decades, and you will need all your resources to unravel their deceptions."

"Do I arm myself, Chief?"

"For two old ladies? Only if you feel they are a threat to your manhood."

"Three old ladies," I corrected. "You forgot Gladys."

This conversation was something of a deception, itself. Hobbes knew I wouldn't go into a strange house on a new case without a weapon of some sort, but he could truthfully say, with Sally to bear witness, that I had not been instructed to carry a weapon. If something went badly wrong, then I would likely be the only one sitting in jail.

Hobbes nodded to Sally, and she left to find her computer, almost bumping into Fred at the doorway.

"'Scuse me," muttered the fireman. "Came in to clean up yer mess." He gathered up the paper plates and napkins, and with his finger, counted the empty beer cans. "Too many. You'll all get beer guts." He let his counting finger swing around to become a pointing finger, targeted at me. "Except for him. He's too fleet of foot to get fat, ha, ha." So Fireman Fred had listened to the discussion with the clients. Well, as a possible assistant in the investigation, he was supposed to, same as Sally — at least when Hobbes had the living room microphones turned on.

"Want some instant coffee, or hot choc'late? I'll heat it up in the microwave." It was all too obvious that he was making up to us, too. We both nodded.

"And then, Fred, will you sit with us?" Hobbes asked.

Fred nodded to the boss, winked at me, and started cleaning up the table.

It occurred to me that Sally had winked at Hobbes earlier, too. It made me feel sad for Charon, who was probably neglected. I shook my head at the thought, and then resolved to wink at nobody for the next twenty-four hours.

"Abel," Hobbes said, interfering with my train of thought.

"Abel," he repeated with a note of irritability, thus regaining my attention. "I suggest you take the Town Car tomorrow." I raised my eyebrow in question. He could drive the van if he wanted to. It had hand controls for the brakes and accelerator that allowed him to drive — and it had a hydraulic lift that could load both him and the wheelchair. He drove it occasionally to prove something to himself, but generally he preferred being chauffeured in the Lincoln.

"It would be more appropriate to the rarified atmosphere of the Borden's neighborhood," he added. Appearance counted in the detective business.

"If you have the opportunity, I would like you to call me each evening on a secure phone, before midnight." I started to interrupt. This was going way too fast. Secure phone? That meant not using their house phones, or even the one in the car. I would have to go to a bar, or a convenience store to call. He held up his hand. "There are already several things about those people that I find disturbing. Especially their avowed reason for hiring me. I suspect it has little to do with what they really want, and they might not even know what that is. There is a sense of danger in their household, either to them or from them. There was much left untold today, and until I know a great deal more about them and their bizarre life, I prefer to keep our reports and conversations secure from eavesdroppers, either human or technological."

The real puzzle to me was there didn't appear to be any real puzzle. Only two things stood out from the meeting, as far as I could see — the size of the fee, and Gloria's comment about "an old, old mystery." Of course, now there was a third; how did the Bordens come to know Katya Ransom?

So, what did they really want from us?

A chime said the microwave was done, and a moment later Fred brought over a tray holding a coffee and two hot chocolates. He silently handed us our drinks, and sat down with his own cup. Fred drinking something hot? This was a strange day.

Hobbes took time to sample Fred's hot chocolate, and asked for some sugar. Then, for the next half-hour, we reviewed some older cases that were similar to our present one. The more successful spirit mediums often used good showmanship more than anything else to make extravagant claims seem real. Frequently, simple tricks were employed and were easy to explain, much to the chagrin of the performer. Some mediums were not so obvious in their flim-flam, so, occasionally we were not able to make a full investigation. Those mediums claimed that they were genuine, simply because we could not prove otherwise.

Chapter 5

Curiously, reviewing the old cases did not help. For one thing the prior subjects had not wanted to be investigated, whereas the Bordens did. For another, they opposed us constantly; the Bordens appeared to give us a free hand.

Sally came in and handed Hobbes a small stack of computer printouts.

"This is no *Lily Dale*," she said. "You can read it over, but you won't find much you don't already know. None of this gives any sense of history prior to five or six years ago, although there are many references to the unsolved murder of Eldred Carpunky."

"What's a lilydale?" Fred asked.

"Two words," I answered for Sally, "Lily and Dale, Lily Dale. Kinda the home of the Spiritualist religion. You can go to meditate, to get in touch with the dead, and maybe even get healed. Right, Chief?" I looked at Hobbes in his wheelchair.

He nodded. "I went there a few months after my accident." He was silent for a moment, reflective. Then he shrugged. "It is a well known place, and well recorded in history, Fred. You may want to visit it someday."

He picked up the printouts and scanned them briefly, then handed them to me.

"I think you'll need to dig much deeper, Sally, certainly into the Chicago venue. Abel will provide you with a debit card, and cash for miscellaneous expenses.

"The Bordens may have had other dealings in Meridian which led them to us, so you may choose to do some local research first. There may be an unexpected feast of meaty stories and rumors about them, but they are from the big city; here, you will more likely find famine. I leave the decision of where to begin to you.

"You did well today, Sally," he added. "Thank you."

I was never sure I understood their relationship, and this was a good example. *What* did she do well today? Search the Internet? Confound the clients? Eat pizza?

Anyway, she seemed to assume she was excused for the evening. She pushed her chair away from the table and then jumped up onto it. She threw her head way back and sniffed the air with delight lighting her face. "It's so fresh," she exclaimed, "So alive!"

In one graceful move, she dropped to the floor and ran to Fred. He had no chance to avoid the kiss on his bald head, nor could he stop her from ruffling the fringe of white hair that rose above his ears and circled down around his neck like a small winter blizzard. She laughed in childlike innocence and then ran from the room.

Hobbes turned to me. "You will no doubt leave early, so I probably won't see you until your return. I remind you to take ample cash. We are on a liberal expense account and you need not scrimp. There is one other option you might consider, even though Sally has already tried it. That is to go first to the downtown offices of the *National Echo* and ask to see their files on Gloria Borden."

"Chief," I said, surprised at the suggestion. "The last time they opened up any of their files to an outsider was the year the Cubs won the pennant. Will they open those files to me? Yeah, when the Cubs win again."

"You have a talent for doing the impossible, Abel. Keep an open mind, and a way may present itself to you. And it doesn't have to be tomorrow."

"You want me to talk to Tom Wilder?"

Hobbes deflected my question with silence. His expression was, as usual, inscrutable. "Remember what I said. I sense danger. Be prudent. Be careful."

"Always am," I replied. He was the boss, and the boss was supposed to be right, but darned if I could figure. He really wanted me to talk to Wilder.

I pushed my chair back. "I think I'll go pack."

"Goodnight, then."

I nodded to him and Fred and left the room, rubbing Fred's head on the way out. He ignored me.

I took the stairs to the second floor and crossed the hallway to my room and its grand view of the Illinois River. My hand was on the doorknob when Sally called me from down the hall. I waited for her.

"Did you read the reports I gave Hobbes?" Up here she sounded uncertain — not quite frightened, but not at all like she had downstairs.

"No, I just glanced over it."

"Eight pages," she whispered. "Eight pages, but twenty-three times the word 'murder' was used."

"That murder, if there was one, was forty years ago."

"That murder," she said. "*That* murder, yes."

Then she pulled my head down and kissed me on the cheek. "I don't like this case." She let me go and dashed back to her room. She turned to look at me once more, and then disappeared inside. I wondered why she was so upset. If there was danger, I was the one going into it.

I turned the knob on my bedroom door, pushed it open, and entered the Lost World. My lost world, really. Hobbes had given it to me when I was thirteen years old, just after he had become my legal guardian. The room would have been his if he had been able to use the stairs –– at fourteen by twenty feet, it was bigger than a lot of living rooms I'd seen. When I first moved in, I'd taken advantage of the space. Space was right. In that first year, I'd built a cardboard simulation of a lunar module. Later, I'd replaced it with one made of wire and papier-mâché that could be broken down into sections for a science fair. It was still here, even after twenty years.

A poster on the wall said, Houston, we have a problem!

Yeah. This Houston –– me, Abel Houston –– had a problem. It was why I threw darts at a board that had Buzz Aldrin's picture for a bull's eye. It's why I never tried to get into the astronaut program.

There's no room for claustrophobia on a space craft.

I shook my head. That was ancient history, and right now I had a job to do.

I sat down on my bed and thought about the case. I'd been warned twice that there was danger ahead. Three times, if I considered the mutilated animals to be tied in somehow, though I figured that was stretching things a bit.

It was not like Sally to react as she did. The odd thing was that no one in this house was supposed to believe in clairvoyance or precognition. It was one of the fundamental precepts of our firm. As a matter of fact, it was our job to disbelieve in them. We did manage to doubt almost everything, but except for Hobbes, the total disbelief just wasn't there. And I wasn't too sure about Hobbes.

While I wouldn't argue against Hobbes' pragmatic approach –– he knew people better than me –– I couldn't see what he saw. Nor did I share in Sally's alarm, though her sense of danger seemed much more exaggerated than his. Anyway, their warnings had seemed definitely along the lines of fortune telling.

Maybe I should get out my tarot cards and read my own future, except I didn't have any. Tarot cards, I mean.

An hour later, I had finished packing. By eleven o'clock, I was in bed. Two minutes after that — two minutes at the most — I was asleep.

I had odd dreams of long red hair and ears with earrings shaped like miniature Boy Scout hatchets.

Judith had said her niece had red hair; she hadn't mentioned earrings.

The next morning, I tossed a few darts at Buzz. Actually it was at my homemade dartboard with this month's *"Astronaut I might have been"* pasted over the bull's eye — Buzz Aldrin in his white space suit with the Apollo Eleven lunar module behind him. One dart nailed him in the foot. I had been seven years old when that picture was taken, just getting caught up in the dream.

I packed equipment and suitcase in the trunk of the Town Car and was backing out onto the street, when I heard a familiar voice.

"Hi, Abel! Where ya goin'?" Richie, the fifteen year old from next door, was delivering the morning *Tribune*. He dropped his headphones down to his neck.

"Near North Chicago, by the lake." I liked the kid. He was a hard worker, eager to make a few bucks. "Grass could use cutting."

"Cool," he said. "I'll do it this afternoon." He glanced at the house next door and lowered his voice. "My step—grandmother's hot about something. What did you do to her?"

"Katya?" I shrugged. "Nothing. Tell me, how do you manage to get along with her?"

"I don't," he said with a grin. "It doesn't take much to get her off, anyway."

He paused for a moment, then added, "Dad says he can do the painting for you next week." Richie and his dad, and his granddad and his granddad's dad, all had spent their childhood in the older house next door; they had all done odd jobs, as boy and man, for their neighbors since the time of the Great Depression.

"I'll be gone for three or four days, Richie. Let Mr. Hobbes know about the painting, will you?"

"Sure," he said. "By the way, the radio said there was a big wreck on Lake Shore Drive. Three or four cars and a bus. Just happened. Buncha people hurt." He grinned at me, "You better be careful up there. Sounds like a dangerous place." He replaced his headphones, listened for a second, and said, "'The Bottomless Pit.' You'd like 'em." He waved goodbye and went on down the sidewalk.

The Bottomless Pit. Sounded like a threat all by itself.

Another warning. And from a kid. I decided I'd put an extra lump of coal in his Christmas stocking this year.

Ten minutes later, I was on I-80 heading east. In an hour and a half I would be on Lake Shore Drive. "Buncha people hurt," the boy had said. I shook my head. Things come in threes. The dead animals had been number one. The downtown accident could have been number two. Maybe I was three. Third time's the charm, and all that. If I were superstitious, I'd be worried, wouldn't I? I put the radio on WFMT and the car on cruise.

I considered the mutilated creatures that had been left on the front porch. Were they warnings or omens? Warnings, I supposed. We weren't supposed to believe in omens.

So what?

A Fine and Private Grave

Danger was my middle name.

Chapter 6

"Six fireplaces," Judith had remarked for some obscure reason, not bragging. "Wood burning, every one." I had driven along the lakefront on Chicago's Outer Drive, and had turned off onto Belleview, per directions. Now, I was looking for the landmark wrought iron fence with its red brick and cement posts, and wondering what she'd meant. Was it to justify Regasmun's claim of a multimillion-dollar house? Or did she simply have something against gas burners, like ours? Maybe she was just cold.

The directions had been precise and a minute after ten, I pulled into a short driveway blocked by a spiked iron gate. I stopped next to a speaker on a pedestal, lowered my window, and waited.

"Yes?" That one word managed to sound throaty, regal, and sensuous. It stopped me cold from ordering a hamburger and fries. I told her who I was, that I was expected. The speaker said, "Please park in back of the house, then walk through the west portico to the north porch. Someone will meet you at the front door."

Wow. I couldn't wait to meet her. The voice sounded familiar, though I couldn't say quite why. I didn't think it belonged to someone I knew.

The gate opened electrically on silent hinges and closed after me. I followed the drive around back, circling a flower garden that left plenty of room for seven or eight cars to parallel park, and stopped in back of a sporty blue Mercedes. I climbed out and stretched to loosen tense muscles and wondered what the top end of that car might be, and where could a guy go to try it out.

"At least a hundred and fifty." A woman in her early thirties, with bright red hair, came from nowhere and laughed at my surprise. "Men always want to know how fast anything is. Cars. Computers. Women. And that's in miles per hour." She nodded at some steps leading from a back door, and lowered her voice. "I'm late. But if you really want to sound reckless, give the speed in kilometers like the Europeans do."

"Marilyn?" I guessed. "The niece?"

"If you're the detective." Her face came alive with her smile, and she offered her hand. Her grip was strong and dry. She would never be a model, I thought, even if she lost twenty or thirty pounds. Among other things, her nose was too long and thin, although I thought that was an appealing contrast to a round and full face.

"More investigator than detective," I said. She had eyes as blue as her aunts' were, but with a warmth and candor I hadn't seen in theirs. Marilyn's eyes seemed to pull me in against my will, and I had to shake my head to break the charm. "Abel Houston, paranormal snoop, ma'am."

"Marilyn Borden, resident student of anthropology and tolerator of the really goofy things that happen here. I'll see you this afternoon. And I really am late." She glanced at my hand and I quickly released hers.

As she drove away in that lovely blue car, I found myself wondering if Judith had told us whether or not her niece was single.

I walked through the west portico to the north porch where I found the front door.

It opened before me, and an elderly woman in a shapeless dress and flat–heeled shoes asked me in with that odd voice I had heard through the gate speaker. The sex appeal –– the sultriness –– didn't extend beyond the tone of her voice. I wondered if she knew how she sounded, and then figured she probably didn't. She let her eyes touch mine for an instant and then looked away. The move was furtive – cautious – like a dog that had been scolded a few times, but didn't know why.

I followed her through the foyer and turned left into a sitting room that boasted two armchairs, a big comfortable couch, and a coffee table covered with ancient *National Geographic* magazines.

"Please wait." Now I knew why she sounded familiar; she reminded me of a telephone answering machine, programmed with ready-made answers.

"You're Gladys, right?" I said as she started to leave. When she hesitated, I continued, "Gladys, you've been with the Bordens a long time, haven't you?"

"We're family, sir. We've been together forty-five years."

"You came here as a child?"

"Went there as a child. I was sixteen."

Judith had said it started "about forty years ago," so I asked where was *there*?

"I don't remember. Don't remember. There was water and a clock. Lot of water and a big clock. Don't remember nothing else." She sighed. "Ain't got Alzheimer's though. Just getting old. Just getting old." After a moment's hesitation, she left the room.

I stared after her. Water and a clock? What was that all about? Like it usually did in a new situation, my mind picked up on the question and rambled away with it.

Did she mean a Chinese Water Torture where a person went crazy counting the seconds while he waited for the next drop of water to fall? Or was she thinking about the clocks in a motion picture shoot— out like *High Noon?* That didn't seem right. I couldn't remember if there was any water in that movie. Not that it mattered. She could have been talking about anything.

About thirty minutes passed as I wandered around the room looking at oil paintings and gilt-edged mirrors. I wasn't much into art, but there was one painting that might have been an original Picasso, and another that could have been a Monet. Two full-length mirrors graced the outer walls, and one of portrait size looked over the room from a darkened corner.

It was while I stood in front of the last one that I impulsively put on my best smile and gave myself a broad wink.

Bored from looking at art and admiring myself, I selected the most comfortable-looking armchair that sported a footstool, sat down, and rested my feet. A moment later, Judith Borden walked in. I jumped up.

She offered a slight smile. "Let's sit where we can talk easily."

I followed her to a small table and held her chair, then sat across from her and studied those remarkable blue eyes. "Your niece looks a great deal like you, you know. Are her father's eyes like hers?" Why had I asked that question?

"No. His are brown. In our ancestry, the blue seems to occur only every other generation. But not always," she amended. "Why? Are you professionally interested in eyes?" Hers were like flint through the thick lenses.

"Excuse me, Miss Borden. I didn't mean to be forward."

"Forget it." She dismissed it with a brief flutter of the hand. "Marilyn's life is her own. I shouldn't interfere. Anyway you are here at our request, and we should humor your inquiries. You have other questions, no doubt, and you would like to investigate our house. You may begin now if you wish."

"Okay." Hobbes and I had decided on a few things to ask when I was alone with any of the clients. "Who had the idea of hiring us?"

"It might have been me. I was worried about Cassius. My brother frequently expressed concern about our mental state and often hinted that we were too old to manage our finances. Avery might have mentioned your firm. As he said, he is uncertain about Cassius' intentions. At any rate, I'm sure Gloria had nothing to say about it. She simply came along."

"Avery didn't sound uncertain about Cassius."

"Oh, I'm sure Avery knew what he was saying."

"And why go all the way to Meridian? There are several competent investigators near here."

"Mr. Hobbes is in Meridian."

That didn't seem like a good enough answer, but I let it pass. Hobbes would probably dig out the real reason before the case was closed.

"Where did you live before you moved to this house?"

"The circumstances that made us move here are not relevant to your investigation. Those reasons were good and have faded with the passage of time. I would not care to resurrect them."

Okay, I thought. Another one for the chief.

I continued, "What happens to your life here if we prove Gloria is a fake?"

"Nothing. Skeptics will be pleased, but that means nothing. Believers will not disbelieve because of you."

"Miss Borden," I said slowly, "We need your honest answer to the next question. It will determine to a great deal how we proceed."

"Then let me ask it for you; it is, after all, the one most obvious."

I nodded, "Go ahead."

"Do I believe in my sister?"

"Uh huh."

"Mr. Houston, when you search this house, you will find many deceits and misdirections, simple tricks and sliding doors, other one-way mirrors — the tools of the trade you might say. Those are the special effects, the glamour of the show, and help bring our customers back even if they do suspect a little trickery. But after you strip away all the pretensions and there is nothing left but what Gloria says, you will decide for yourself.

"When there are just the words of Eldred Carpunky through Gloria, you will believe!"

One thing was for sure, Judith believed — or believed she believed, and with passion. Unless of course, she was lying.

"There is one more thing, Miss Borden, and it may not be relevant to our investigation, but I am curious about your sister and Katya Ransom."

Judith gave me one of her rare smiles, "That vile, evil woman brought her cat to one of Gloria's meetings and demanded that Eldred bring her deceased husband here. She wanted to give him a piece of her mind, but do you know what Eldred said?"

I shook my head.

"He said her husband wouldn't come into the same room with her, and that she should live forever so that he would never have to see any part of her. Katya was very unhappy, and quite angry with Gloria, but she still wrote out a check and gave it to Avery. Then, she said to her cat, 'Out, Harmless, before I do something they will regret,' and then she left, slamming the door with great force."

We talked for a few more minutes — Judith suddenly reserved — until she said it was noon and time for lunch; I followed her into the dining room.

I didn't know what I expected in a house that was worth several million dollars, but it wasn't poached orange roughy nor tomatoes stuffed with thin spaghetti, nor was it blackberries covered with a thick strawberry puree. I had two helpings of everything, and was thinking of trading our Fred for their cook, until I realized the cook must be Gladys.

As I finished, and while Judith still picked at her food, Gloria entered. This time, she was dressed in light gray, and without a veil. Her hair, like her sister's, was naturally red, but its brightness suggested the color was enhanced. Maybe at seventy-five, it was turning gray, but I supposed that was none of my business.

She took some fish and blackberries, which she spooned together, but skipped the tomatoes. I sat in silence while she ate. I sipped my coffee. When Judith got up to leave, Gloria said, "Tonight, eight o'clock."

Judith nodded and excused herself. Gloria finished her meal in quiet concentration, and then politely touched her napkin to each corner of her mouth. As she folded the napkin and placed it on the table, her eyes met mine and for the first time she seemed to see me.

It was as though she had known I was present, but just now realized it. She spoke quietly. "I'm glad you are here, Abel. In the Bible, Abel was killed by his brother Cain. May I call you Abel?" Her warm, friendly eyes sought acknowledgement, and found it. "Of course I may." She rose and walked around the table to pour me fresh coffee. A faint hint of some exotic perfume followed her, and I wondered what she must have been like fifty years ago. I picked up the cup, and felt its warmth in my hands.

"Eldred wants to talk to you, Abel," she said without preamble.

A bit of hot coffee sloshed over the rim of the cup, and I hurriedly placed it in its saucer. "Eldred?" The vision of a skull covered with rotted skin appeared for an instant.

"Not like that," she said, seeing my expression. "He's all energy now, and fire, and dream. When you see him, you'll find him beautiful, as I do."

An unnatural shiver began in my chest.

"He wants you to be part of a sitting tonight so he can talk to you. He wants you to decide for yourself whether or not he is genuine, and the only way is through a sitting. Judith is arranging it. We three, and Avery, Cassius, and Gladys will be there. Eldred will be the seventh guest.

"He wants showmanship from us tonight, my dear. He loves the candles and the soft music and the incense, and tonight the atmosphere will be special beyond the normal. He wants you to test him. To find the real and the not real. Then perhaps you'll be ready for Monday, when you and he can have a private meeting."

It took a moment for the idea of a second meeting to sink in –– we hadn't had a first yet. "Eldred and I, alone? I thought he wouldn't talk to anyone but you."

"Oh, I will have to be there, as I will tonight, but you and he will be alone in a sense as I neither know nor remember what he says through me. Tonight, I'll record the sitting on our recorder and listen to what he says later. But he doesn't want me to know what he'll say to you on Monday, so for that sitting the recorder will be off." She stood again. "Until later, dear Abel," she said. Then she, too, left the room.

Chapter 7

I drank more of my coffee and considered what had just been said. Mostly, I had found myself thinking of Eldred as if he was real. That kind of reaction was as rare for me as it was for Hobbes. In our line of work, ghosts usually stayed ghosts. They had no substance except for whatever those willing to believe in them thought they could see.

Left alone, I decided to take an unguided tour of the first floor, at least as much as I could. Going back to the foyer where I'd first met Gladys seemed like a good place to start. This time I could take my time going through it and see what I'd missed. So I wandered back to the front door. When I'd first been invited in, Gladys took me left to the sitting room. Then, I had only briefly noticed the stairway going up, and the wide hallway next to it that led to the back of the house. Now I found it most curious, but even more mysterious was the long corridor to the right that passed through two four-foot wide archways.

I followed the same wide hallway that had taken us to the dining room, and I supposed would also reach the kitchen and the utility side of the house. Since I'd already seen the sitting room, I followed the corridor through the first archway and found hall closets to the right and a closed door to the left. The closed door opened into the library, which showed signs of use — many books but no TV. If Gloria had kept the same bedroom for forty years, it would be right above here. About twelve feet ahead, the second arch enclosed double doors that begged me to slide them open and let them disappear into the walls.

I reached out to honor their request when Judith's voice stopped me.

"Yes," she said dryly. "You have the freedom as a hired investigator to go where curiosity leads you. That's the room where we have the sittings, the spirit room. You can go in now, if you desire. I wonder, though, if you would find it better to wait until after this evening's sitting to examine the room. Gloria's show is much more effective when you are unprepared for the mysteries that surround it. You could still set up your cameras and recorders a few minutes before we start, as long as you don't look around too closely." She had a smugness in her tone that annoyed me.

"In the meantime you can bring your equipment into the library, and I will have Gladys show you to a guest room."

"Thanks," I said. "But if it's all the same to you, I'd rather not waste any time. If you want me to prove anything tonight, I'll need to be prepared. I promise to be as unobtrusive as possible. I do want to enjoy the show."

"Very well. I'll have Gladys take you upstairs whenever you are ready."

"That, she can do right now," I said. "Ask her to show me the way to the back door, too, so I can bring my equipment in."

A few minutes later, I knew where my bedroom and bathroom were, and had followed Gladys out to my car. I suspected by her nervousness that she had something on her mind, so I took my time with the things in the trunk.

Finally, she blurted out, "She ain't goin' to jail, is she?" Wide-eyed, frightened, her earlier professional housekeeper's voice gone, she sounded more eighteen than eighty.

"Gloria?" She didn't seem to hear me. "What for?" Go to jail for claiming to talk to a spirit? Not likely. Maybe she was talking about Judith.

"You know, back then, when she was in love, an' he weren't. You know." Her eyes pleaded with me.

"Who do you mean, Gladys?"

"You are so kind, and so, so smart. You'll help 'er, won't you? She wouldn't hurt no one!" Suddenly, she turned and ran back into the house.

I stared after her, and then slowly hefted luggage out of the trunk. I wished Hobbes were here.

With the equipment stacked in the library and my suitcases upstairs, I took a preliminary look at the spirit room. No less than sixteen feet wide and thirty long, it still seemed remarkably intimate. Both ends boasted brick fireplaces — wood burning, with mantels of jade colored marble. Windows flanked the one on the south end and mirrors the other. Dark leather couches with dim lamps on cocktail tables next to them faced each fireplace. Near one end, an upright ebony piano sat, polished to a high gloss and shimmering in the light from the front windows.

A round red mahogany table and six upholstered chairs dominated the room, a little off center to balance the piano's presence.. The chairs featured oversized casters on their legs, probably to make them easy to move on the plush carpet concealing all but the outer edges of the polished hard oak floor. Full-length thick velvet curtains covered the four windows on the long outer wall.

Six portrait-sized gilt mirrors lined the long inside wall; two more mirrors adorned the adjacent wall, one on each side of the fireplace in lieu of windows. They all looked like the small mirror in the sitting room. Behind them, the walls were covered with gray satin wallpaper flecked with gold.

Overall, the effect was somber, serious, and lavish — the ideal atmosphere for people who wanted to believe in séances.

It was time to earn my pay.

"This must be the paranormal snoop doing his paranormal snooping." The voice was cheerful, and I turned to see Marilyn in the doorway. She stepped to me and offered her hand.

I took it and held it too long. "The tolerator," I said, and because I could think of nothing else, added, "In kilometers per hour, two hundred and seventy."

She laughed, a great boisterous sound. "You are reckless," and slowly withdrew her hand.

"I'm going to test the room for devices. Stay and I'll show you some of my best-kept secrets. And you can call me Abel."

"Me, Marilyn." She became somber then and added, "I'd be happy to stay."

I retrieved one of my cases from the library and opened it.

"Marilyn," I said, "You know I'm here pretty much to prove your aunt is a fake."

She nodded. "When I was in college, I wrote a paper on channeling –– on spirits using a live body to talk to the living. Aunt Gloria was the subject, and Eldred was the spirit. I transcribed a séance, and, with Aunt Gloria's approval, submitted it as part of the paper." She studied a piece of my equipment for a few seconds, and then went on. "I attempted to give some logical explanations for what happened, but I have to admit they were pretty feeble. As near as I could tell, there wasn't any scientific basis in what she was doing, but neither was it all hocus–pocus."

She held up my mirror analyzer, "Home made?"

"Patent applied for."

"Naturally." She studied it some more. "It should be worth a fortune."

"Enough to take you out to dinner?"

"Maybe. Do you know what grade I got on the paper?"

"B–plus?"

"D–minus. Worst grade I ever got. But I was a freshman then, and a long way from becoming an anthropologist. My later reports were better, but I've never tried to investigate her again."

"Why not?"

"I suppose it's too close to home, Abel. But, I am a scientist, and I'd still like to know the truth, one way or another."

"Truth?" I shook my head. "I'm just looking for proof. It's much easier to find, and it can be manipulated so that people think it is the truth."

"A little cynical, are we?"

"Sometimes," I acknowledged. "But about Gloria. It's this way, Marilyn. I don't know whether she really talks to a dead man, but I intend to find out, or come real close. If she turns out to be a phony, will that bother you? I mean, will it bother you a lot?"

"Do your best," was all she said.

She watched with a friendly sort of curiosity as I began setting up my test equipment. First, I pulled out a simple home-made device: a krypton beam flashlight and light meter fastened together and attached to the swivel mount of a tripod. "This will establish a reference for light reflected from a mirror," I explained. I placed the reference mirror on the floor directly under the flashlight, and then turned on the light. I cranked the assembly down until it was forty inches directly above the mirror and read the light meter.

"Thirty six," I said. "That's my reference number. Any standard mirror would reflect about that much light at the same distance from the flashlight, but a one-way mirror will pass some of the light through to whomever's in back of it, so it will reflect that much less."

"So you can tell if there are any hidden rooms where an accomplice might observe and do things on cue?"

"Right. Now, watch." I swiveled the apparatus from the vertical to the horizontal position and set it up forty inches back from the first of the six mirrors along the inner wall. Then, I had Marilyn read the meter.

"Thirty five," she said. "What kind of deviation would tell you it's a one-way mirror?"

I shrugged, "Thirty two or less."

The next five were also okay, but I hadn't expected much from them because my earlier glance into the library –– which was on the other side of the wall –– showed nothing but bookcases opposite the mirrors. I expected something from the ones that flanked the fireplace because there seemed to be some room behind them, but I was surprised. Both were honest-to-goodness, the real thing. Now, that was annoying. I had expected at least one trick mirror.

I glanced at Marilyn, but she only looked interested, not surprised.

I set up the other test instruments one by one and conducted the standard checks: the fireplaces for remote igniters, the table and chairs for hidden switches, the couches, the drapes — everything. For the next two or three hours, I searched. I found nothing, although earlier it had seemed to me that Judith thought I would.

"I didn't expect you to," was all Marilyn had to say about my search not turning up an obvious sign of trickery. A few minutes later she added, "It's dinnertime. Why don't we stop for now?"

Frustration gnawed at me. When was a hoax not a hoax? Answer: when no rational explanation could be found. Of course, I hadn't yet seen the hoax, had I? Judith was right. I should have waited for the Gloria Show.

She had said it would begin after supper when everyone was here. In the meantime, I was to get my cameras and such ready, although I had a nagging feeling they wouldn't do me a lot of good.

Chapter 8

Stir-fried calamari was the main course for dinner. I probably would have liked it more if I hadn't known what it was. Regasmun came in at seven when salad was just being served; he chose a seat at the far end of the table. He picked at his food, obviously annoyed at being summoned for an unscheduled sitting. Cassius Borden came in a few minutes later. He stopped to kiss Judith on the cheek, then surveyed the rest of the table. He waved at Marilyn who said "Daddy," without any particular expression, then chose a chair next to mine. Before sitting, he offered me his hand; it was cool and slightly damp, but the grip was strong.

Cassius was sixty, they had said. His waistline was probably more than he wanted, and his face was florid — as if he had enjoyed too much rich food and drink. He looked his age. A strong smell of cigar smoke reached out and touched everyone, but he offered no apology. Still, he seemed physically fit and self-assured as if he lifted weights, or played racquetball. His brown-going-gray hair was styled, though his moustache grew wild and untamed in a way that gave the man a devil-may-care look. His eyes were brown behind wire-rimmed glasses. He was the kind of guy you could like or dislike, depending.

"Gloria never eats before a sitting," he said, "in case you wondered where she was. Did you know that?"

"Not for sure," I answered and grinned. "But some mediums say an empty stomach helps them relate to the dead."

"I bet you've seen a lot of them — mediums I mean, not the dead."

"A few of both," I admitted.

"None of them like Gloria, I'll wager."

"I don't know, Mr. Borden. I haven't seen her in action."

He looked pained. "The only man here old enough to be called Mister is Regasmun. I'd still like to be thought of as a kid. Would you object to first names?"

"Not if you'll tell me more about your sister."

"Okay, Abel. How about I tell you how she begins her séance?"

"Great," I said, leaning back.

As we talked, I found myself puzzled by the picture Avery and Judith had painted of him. For one thing, he spoke of his sisters with respect for their intelligence, not as if they were becoming incompetent. For another, he didn't seem much concerned about their money. At one point, Cassius told me, "I really do have their best interests at heart you know, regardless of what they say."

I decided to let Hobbes figure out the discrepancy between what we had been told and what I was hearing now.

"I'm curious," he said. "If I can be so bold as to ask, why do you work for Hobbes? I mean, how do you

64

fit into this charade? You know it's all fake. One hundred percent phony."

"Is it?" I replied. "All phony? I don't know that yet. Hobbes says it is and he's paying me to prove he's right, and he's always been right, but maybe someday he won't be."

Cassius paused to taste his chocolate mousse and answered slowly, "Yet you're doing your damnedest to help him prove he's right."

I studied the scalloped edging where the walls met the ceiling. "I've got to get past the frauds and hoaxes first. So I work for Hobbes, and we do pretty well together. When I was a boy..." I was about to tell him about Mad Molly Beecher and the tunnels under Meridian State Hospital, but that would have led to talk about the coven and the sacrifices. All of that happened over twenty years ago and was all too personal to tell to someone I barely knew. So I finished kind of lamely, "Things happened that brought us together."

"Yeah?"

"When I find something that is truly supernatural, I'll tell you about it. I'll tell everybody."

Cassius shrugged. "Well, good luck. Just keep in mind that everything you see and hear tonight is staged."

"Do you know how it's done?"

"Not a clue."

"Then how do you know it's staged?"

"How could it be real?"

That was the question, wasn't it?

The faint chime of a silver bell ended our discussion, and then Cassius, Judith, Avery, and I left the dining room in a quiet sort of anticipation. We were joined in the hall by Gladys. She said that Marilyn had stayed behind to clean up the kitchen.

The hallway seemed cooler than it had earlier; fans on the high ceiling ran on whisper mode and stirred air already chilled by air conditioning. Indirect lighting dimmed slowly as we passed the stairs and the closed library doors to enter the spirit room, Judith leading the way.

She placed her cold hand on my arm and pushed me gently to a chair on the side of the table nearest the door. She allowed Cassius to seat her in the one next to me, to my left, and then he went to what I immediately thought of as the foot of the table, even though the table was round. Next to him, across from me, was Gladys, and to her left was Avery. The chair between him and me was empty, waiting for Gloria.

"Give me a minute," I said to Judith as I went to check my equipment. Marilyn had told me that nothing must be placed on the table, so I had made use of the mantels at each end of the room for the video recorder and the infrared and ultraviolet cameras. The video I turned on to run continuously. I would trigger the cameras by pressing my heels together, engaging a magnetic switch that would send a signal to the cameras telling them to start taking pictures in rapid sequence as long as my heels touched. An audio recorder and a separate broadband radio receiver stood on tripods a respectful distance from the table. Satisfied, I returned to my chair.

In the faint light, I saw that both women had chosen to wear sweaters, and again I noticed the coolness of the air. Although Avery wore a suit and still looked annoyed, Cassius appeared comfortable in a polo shirt that left his arms bare. Briefly, Gladys made eye contact with me, her expression worried, questioning. I had no answer for her; I didn't understand the question.

Speakers in the ceiling allowed a piano concerto by Mozart to caress the walls and table and us, the soft tones of music taking the edge off a growing tension. The hallway went dark and the draperies at the windows closed, blocking the feeble light from the street. Our dim lamps grew dimmer and then expired, leaving only afterimages that, for a moment, haunted the room almost prophetically.

In the darkness and soft music, the chilled air had its effect on me. I shivered and then became intensely aware of smells: Judith's expensive perfume, Gladys' cologne, Cassius' cigars. Oddly familiar sounds tugged at my hearing, slightly distorted by the music: the shuffling of feet on the carpet, a brief rhythmical tapping of a finger against the table, someone whispering, "Pictures, yes, I know...," a subtle cough, the repeated clearing of someone's throat — a sudden quick sobbing. I strained to focus on that last sound but couldn't tell where it came from, or if it were man or woman. It was not repeated.

A faint glow of light turned all eyes to the hallway. We watched as a candelabra with seven spikes and lighted candles seemed to float toward us. Only the white hand on the base of the candelabra let us know there was a person behind it. Even when she entered the room, the barely visible black veil and black lace gown made her into a spectral illusion; the hand and an occasional glimpse of a bare foot were all that linked her to our real world. She moved to the head of the table, leaned forward and gently placed the candelabra in its center. Avery slipped from his seat and held her chair as she made a gracious bow and lowered herself effortlessly into it. In the soft light, with her hands in her lap and her midnight-colored garments, she became more shadow than substance — a dark spirit, or a spirit in darkness. I caught my breath. Cassius had tried to prepare me for her entrance, but he had done a lousy job.

The central candle — the tallest one, flickered suddenly and sputtered. A hush settled on the room. Even the music stopped. Belatedly, I remembered my still cameras and triggered them with my heels. The silent, flash-less electronic gear should catch anything spectral and record it. In theory, at least, I would be able to retrieve the images immediately after the sitting and view them on my computer's screen.

"Eldred!" Gloria's voice was clear as crystal, without resonance. "Are you here?" The candle — only that center candle — sputtered again. "Will you talk to us?"

A long moment passed, then we heard a tap — faint, but unmistakable — from under the table, and then a second. I resisted the foolish urge to look; I knew I would find nothing. Two taps meant "yes." I found I had been holding my breath, and released it.

"Do you know yet who murdered you?" Cassius had said Gloria always asked that question, and always got the same answer: one tap, no. She continued, "Is there someone here you wish to talk to?" Two quick taps. "Who?" she asked. A candle to the left of the tall candle flickered. "Abel Houston?" Two more taps. "Very well."

To us she said, "Please place your hands on the table." We complied, and she continued, "Take the hand of the person next to you."

Judith captured my left hand in an icy grasp that felt strong as iron; Gloria placed her left hand over my right in a warm, soft, but just as inflexible grip. For a panicky moment I felt trapped, unable to move. It took a small effort of will to remember that these were two elderly women whose strength could be no match for mine. Nevertheless, for an instant, the old claustrophobia had placed a more powerful hand than either of theirs around my chest, and the darkness and the shadows on the walls had assumed ominous proportions.

A surge of energy, like electricity, moved through me and seemed to circle the table, passing several times. Suddenly, six of the candles went out, leaving only the one in the center with its hesitant, uncertain fire.

"Look at the light," Gloria whispered, the pitch of her voice dropping, losing its feminine quality. "Look into its heart. Concentrate. Let images form. Envision the spirit of the flame. Allow it to come to you."

The power of suggestion, I thought. She had great powers of suggestion.

The room seemed to grow even colder. I shivered.

A face was forming within the fire: young, manly, dark eyes, temples pulsing with life. It danced around the candle's wick, searching; its gaze passing from face to face, pausing at each, moving on. It stopped on mine. Then the flame went out. The image burned in my eyes for a few seconds, a bright blue against a flashing yellow background. Slowly it faded, to be replaced by a soft gentle cry from Gloria. It was like a faint siren, rising only once before falling into a deep masculine tone. The hand she held over mine suddenly relaxed, then just as quickly reasserted itself. The darkness was complete; that small cough came again and was followed by a sob that now sounded forlorn, abandoned. The wood in both fireplaces ignited, and grotesque shadows played across the room.

"I am dead. Why am I dead?" The voice came suddenly, hollow and hopeless. Though I was anticipating the experience, it wasn't what I expected. Special effects aside, there was something real here.

Judith answered. "Someone is here to talk with you, Eldred."

"Abel?" the voice said. Gloria's but not Gloria's.

I cleared my throat, "I'm here."

"Do you know who we are?"

I had expected a voice like something from an old movie — creepy, otherworldly, even hokey. This was more normal, relaxed and confident. Of course, I reflected, they'd had forty years to work on it.

"I'm not sure." We?

"We are Eldred and Gloria. For this time, we are one. We will answer your questions so far as we are able."

"Can you show yourself, Eldred? Just you alone?" I was ready to click my heels together.

"You see us."

In a way I did. With the aid of the firelight, I could see that Gloria's posture had taken on subtle changes. Her back was slightly hunched; her head tilted back, resting against the chair. Her veil seemed, for the moment, less than black. Belatedly, I brought my heels together as I would remember to do very few times that night.

"Who are you, Eldred? Is Eldred your real name?"

"Eldred is Eldred."

I needed better answers, or better questions. I was supposedly talking to a ghost. A better question. How about this? "Why do you want to talk to me?"

"We want to talk of Eldred's death. We want you and your friend to find out who killed us. We have waited too long. Our time is short."

Hobbes will love this, I thought. And maybe he was right about danger.

"Then I need details," I said. "Tell me about your... about the death."

The answer was slow in coming, and painful to hear.

"Eldred loved someone. Someone loved Eldred. Another loved Eldred, too, and went with Eldred.

71

Someone was angry. Someone was jealous. Eldred saw the ax and laughed. Someone Eldred loved saw the ax, too — saw a basement, saw water, saw a clock. Someone raised the ax high, raised the ax high, raised the ax high... Eldred remembers nothing else."

Water and clock? Who else had mentioned water and a clock? Gladys?

The voice continued, "We believe the murderer is here, in this room. We cannot give a name above another. Wait." For a few minutes there was nothing but eerie silence. I listened for the sob but didn't hear it. The voice returned, "We think we are finished. We will part now."

Chapter 9

"Don't go," I said hastily. Maybe he was done, but I wasn't. "I have only two more questions."

There was another long pause, then, "Very well, but we are tired. Speak quickly."

"Why us? Why ask Hobbes and me to come here? We're a long way from home." As the ghost flies, I thought.

"Yes. Far away, far away you were then. The Houston spirit had yet to descend. The Hobbes spirit was young. Now it is different. You are both not far away."

"Far away from what?"

"From me. From dying. From death."

"That tells me nothing. So far you've told me nothing," I wanted to take Gloria by the shoulders and shake something out of her.

"You will know when you know."

It's, or whoever's, cryptic answers were starting to annoy me. I made one more plea, "Tell me about Eldred before he was killed. Where was he born? Where did he live? What did he do?"

When it answered, the voice had lost some cohesion — its maleness disappearing, Gloria's personality returning. "You know the wheres. We laid bricks. We must go now."

The sitting was over. I sat in the near-darkness and studied each face briefly. With the exception of

Gladys, who looked confused, and Gloria who seemed to be coming out of a trance, they all held carefully neutral expressions.

Cassius Borden broke the silence. "If that doesn't prove she's crazy, I don't know what will." It was one of those moments when I didn't like him.

"Turn some lights on, Cassius," Judith said in a flat voice.

"Pictures," I heard Gladys mutter. "I have pictures of a clock..."

The lights came on.

"I need a drink," Regasmun said to nobody in particular. "Maybe two." He stood up, pushed his chair in, and left the room.

"I'm going out for a cigar," Cassius said. "Care to come along?" I shook my head, and he disappeared down the hallway toward the front door.

Judith told me Gloria needed to rest, and they, too, left.

"It'll help you to help 'er if I find them, won't it?" Gladys looked at me, her eyes big and luminous.

"The pictures?"

"Yes, yes. Pictures. I'll look for them. But it's been so long. It will take time, much time. Where are they? Where are they?" She became introspective as if searching memories. "I'll start looking now."

She walked to the door, talking to herself. I could still hear her as she disappeared down the long hallway.

I felt like I'd just played a bit part in a short third act of a bad melodrama.

I gathered up my equipment and took it to the library and locked it in its cases. I wasn't worried about security; I doubted that anyone here could get by the professional locks that protected the cases. Besides, I felt an itching in my palms that told me I was missing something. I needed to talk to Hobbes soon. I was missing something important.

My hand was still itching as I took the stairs two at a time up to my room. I traded my jacket and tie for a shoulder holster and a red *Bears* windbreaker. It was after ten, cooling off, and I had to walk four blocks to get to the nearest phone at a place called *Toby's*. Marilyn had suggested it earlier, laughing at my professional caution about listeners on an extension, or someone tuning in on my cell phone transmission.

Then, she gave me a guest entry code for the front door that would be good until two a.m., and said walking might be quicker than driving because of the parking problem. At that time, walking in the late evening with a cool lake breeze at my back had seemed a good idea. Now I wasn't so sure, and it was a bit of reassurance to have the thirty-two Beretta Tomcat in my shoulder holster.

According to the grandfather clock in the foyer, it was ten after ten as I let myself out. The gate opened easily and closed quietly behind me. Traffic on Belleview didn't seem bad for a Saturday night — yes, I thought, it had been only yesterday when we were hired. It seemed a lot longer. Impatient drivers honked as they passed both ways with a casual disregard for speed and came perilously close to the few cars parked by the street. A convertible with four enthusiastic teenagers and squealing tires turned into the driveway next door and disappeared through the gate. A Volvo waited stoically at the curb, windows down, the glow of a cigarette briefly turning its insides a soft red.

I walked one block west and had just turned left onto a side street that led to *Toby's,* when I heard what sounded like the subdued closing of a car door. I stepped back a few feet so I could see up and down Belleview, but only the Volvo was there, yard lights reflecting against its closed windows. Nobody in sight. I didn't see the light from the cigarette anymore. But maybe that was just because I was further away. Or maybe the guy had finally gone into one of the houses. I stood for a few more moments to assure myself that nobody was following, then resumed my walk.

Toby's was a pleasant neighborhood bar — busy and smoky, TV not too loud, customers loosened up by drink and familiar camaraderie. Nobody but the bartender paid any attention to me as I ordered a Coke and asked where the pay phone was. "Just to the right of the door," he said, "by the coat racks."

I looked over and saw there were two coat racks. Good, I could stand behind them and see whoever came in after me — not that I really thought I was being followed. Watching was just habit.

It was also out of habit that I called collect. It annoyed Hobbes when I didn't use my calling card, which he thought was cheaper. He answered on the fourth ring, and after a short pause told the operator that yes, he would accept the charges, and we were connected.

"Abel?"

"Good evening, Chief. Have you had supper yet?"

"Ham sandwiches, three hours ago. Have you anything worth reporting?"

"We had stir-fried calamari, Chief, but it would have been better with a white wine sauce."

"No doubt. Is that all you have?"

"No sir. I have many facts and fables, as well as impressions, to report. You may want to tape this."

"Very well."

A small man, looking not unlike a leprechaun in a green jacket and hat, walked in and took a seat at the bar. It seemed odd to see a man carrying a box of tissues into a tavern, but he didn't seem the least bit self-conscious about it. He ordered something and then looked over the customers, his eyes meeting mine for a moment.

He smiled and waved. I waved back half-heartedly. Why, I'm not sure. Maybe a response to some deep-seated sense of courtesy. Hobbes came back on the phone, "Recording, Abel. Continue."

The leprechaun lit a cigarette. "Uh, yes boss," I said. "Do you want me to summarize it first, or give you everything as it happened?"

"Tell me everything from the beginning. I'll interrupt for clarification when needed."

Okay," I said. "It was a dark and stormy night..."

"Abel Houston," he cut in very slowly. The little man in green placed the box of tissues on the bar, removed one and blew his nose. He stuffed the used tissue into a jacket pocket. He pointed the box of tissues at me, as if offering me one.

I turned my face to the wall and cupped my hand around the mouthpiece, and spoke softly. "I pulled up to their gate at ten-thirty this morning, about twelve hours ago."

Hobbes, being a detective, detected the change in my voice, and interrupted again. "Are you being observed?"

"I don't know." I described the situation and added, "It all may sound a bit paranoid, but my hand's still itching."

"Your itching hand has been a reliable warning, Abel. If you suddenly feel you have to hang up, do so. You can call from some other place."

I looked back at the bar. "I don't think I'll need to. He's gone."

My boss was silent for a long moment. "I advise you to be careful about your back, Abel. There may be no cause for alarm, or there may be cause. Now, you said ten-thirty?"

Reporting to Hobbes was no easy process. He wanted details — not just what was said, but how, and why, and sometimes where and when. If he asked me to repeat something I was quoting, it wasn't because he doubted my memory, but because he wanted the tone of voice — the emotion the person was feeling, to come through.

When dealing with reports of the occult and the supernatural, how words were expressed was often more important than the words themselves.

On occasion, the retelling of a fifteen-minute happening might take two hours or so. Not this time, though. We didn't always go into such detail when on the phone, and besides, I had this feeling I had missed something. He seemed tobe aware of it, so he was settling for the skin of the report. Meat and bones could come when I was back home.

Nevertheless, it took time, and often during the next hour, I saw the bartender shake his head in puzzlement, but I barely noticed the ebb and flow of the people and sounds around me. Hobbes wanted to know what Marilyn was late for, why she had chosen anthropology, if the Mercedes was hers; why was Gladys so agitated, where was the water and the clock, what color were her eyes? And so on.

He asked if I'd seen all six fireplaces; I hadn't yet, only three -- the two in the spirit room and the one in my bedroom. Did I believe Judith believed in Gloria? Yes and no. Did Gloria think she was talking to Eldred? I thought so. Did I know who Gladys was worried about? Not for sure.

About the spirit room, he asked if effects like the sputtering and extinguishing of the candles were credible. I said he'd have to see them for himself.

Those were all minor details in the report. The tougher questions would come when we got to the séance, though the part about the sobbing seemed to concern him.

Once into my report on the sitting, he let me go through it uninterrupted, then he asked me to repeat the conversation. Hobbes was surprised by the use of the collective pronoun "we" and as confused as I was about the "someones," the "wheres," and the "laid bricks." So far, my report had gone smoothly and comfortably. Then, I told him about Gladys and the pictures.

"Tell me again, Abel," his words were hard enough to send sparks through the telephone line, "About the sobbing."

I described the sounds and listened to their sadness and hopelessness as they echoed through my mind and ground into my gut. People sobbed through sittings.

It happened.

For some, it was an emotional time because they thought they were contacting a loved one. That wasn't the case here. There wasn't any loved one. And the sobs were all wrong. They had the sound of desperation, of final measures, of impending... something. The pictures. "Chief..."

"You must go *now*, Abel!!! Run!!! Get her to safety!"

Chapter 10

I slammed the phone down and headed to the door. Run! A minute a block — four blocks — four minutes, and maybe too late already. I could have made it in four minutes, too, except that when I turned onto Belleview, the low moan of a warning siren and a spotlight brought me up short.

"Okay, Cousin, take it easy," the amplified voice of authority said, and a squad car pulled up to the curb beside me. I stood there catching my breath, my hands at my side, as two cops got out and walked up, hands on the grips of holstered automatics. "Bad time of night to be out jogging, ain't it? Not that you're dressed proper for running or anything." It was the voice from the loud speaker, without the loud speaker, casual, friendly. "You live around here?"

"I'm staying with the Bordens, officer. The house with the spiked iron fence."

"Most people around here know about the Bordens, Cousin, and where they live. Now, put your hands on the roof of the car, please. Spread your legs. That's it. Check him, Jack."

Jack found my pistol immediately. "I have a license," I volunteered. "I'm a private detective." Not that I wanted to make a big deal about the license, but mentioning it seemed appropriate. He carefully took the Beretta from its holster and stepped back.

"Yeah," he said. "And you spend nights running down side streets in a high class neighborhood. What do you think, Al?"

"Let's see your license, Cousin."

I carefully took out my billfold and opened it. "Look, Officers, I need to get to the Bordens' house as soon as possible. It's very important. Anybody there can vouch for me."

"Do you mind a little ride?"

I looked at the squad car with its caged back seat. "If you don't mind, I'd rather walk. Claustrophobic. You understand?" I could feel my skin turning clammy.

Al looked at me thoughtfully. "Okay, Cuz. I'll walk with you. Jack, you bring the car."

I nodded and said, "Thanks." Al and I walked the final block; Jack followed close behind without using the flashing lights on the squad car. We stopped at the gate, and Jack parked in the driveway by the speaker and said something into it. We waited, but nobody responded. It was past midnight, but Gladys would have answered if she were able to. I felt a lead knot forming in the pit of my stomach. Why didn't she answer?

"They gave me a code," I said, seeing the illuminated keypad. I punched in the four digits Marilyn had given me, but nothing happened. I realized she'd probably programmed the front door only, thinking that Gladys would open the gate for me. "Can you call from your car? I have the number."

"No," Al said. "I don't think we want to disturb the good people this time of night, not yet, anyway." He sounded apologetic. "Look at the situation from our point of view, it's after midnight, and you were armed and running. Now, I have to ask you to get in the car. We'll take a ride downtown and get this all straightened out."

A vision of jail cells, small and confining, swept over me. I looked in frustration at the house, so close, and thought, *What about Gladys? Why didn't she answer?* I glanced at my watch. Ten minutes had been lost. Maybe I was already too late. "Listen, officers," I was thinking fast. There had to be a way around them. "I work for Car'l Hobbes. You could call him."

Jack started to write the name down, "Is that with a 'K' or a 'C'?"

I spelled it out.

He looked up at me, "What's the apostrophe for?"

"He never says. The phone number is..."

"Don't matter. You can call him from downtown."

"But I need to talk to someone in that house right now!"

"Sorry, Cuz, but that's the procedure around here. It'll all be cleared up come morning."

I didn't know what else to say.

Officer Al took my arm and guided me to the squad car.

Rescue came in a surprising form –– a voice from out of nowhere. "Hi, Al! Hi, Jack! Now what would you lads be doing now with me bosom buddy?"

It was the guy from the bar, the little guy in the green jacket and green hat. He walked up to us and stopped, just out of the brighter lights, hat perched jauntily on top of curly brown hair, hands on his hips.

"What the hell do you want?" Jack asked.

"Now listen, me boy," the little man sounded offended. "I'm watching out for me old friend Abel Houston here. We go back a long way together now." All the way to Toby's, I thought, and studied him. I didn't know what he was up to, though I had a vague idea. And he might get me into the house.

"You know me, and you know I would not be lying when I say me friend has business in this house. I say, too, that those living within would appreciate your call, even if you do awaken them." He beamed at the cops and nodded.

Al sighed deeply. "I don't know what you're doing here, Green. I don't think I want to know. But, okay. We'll call."

"That's me boy. And you can use me cell phone." He took it from his belt and offered it to Officer Al.

I told the policeman the number, and a few minutes later the gate opened. I stopped Jack as he turned to leave, and held out my hand. He retrieved my pistol from the car and handed it to me. "No hard feelings?"

"None," I said. "I know how it is."

The little green man gave me his card and said he'd be in touch. The card read: *Forrest Green, Ace Reporter, National Echo,* and gave five telephone numbers: office, home, cellular, fax, and pager. Well, I thought, the plot thickens. Unless the *Echo* had a clairvoyant reporter on its staff, someone from the house had called them. There was no other connection between Forrest Green and Tom Wilder, other than the obvious. Wilder was Green's boss. Yet there was always room for some other nefarious goings on when it came to sorting this mystery out. I'd let Hobbes think that through.

When I got to the house, Marilyn met me at the door. She told me that Judith and Gloria were sleeping and that the men had left before midnight. "I need to see Gladys right away," I said.

"Sure." Marilyn responded. "It's only half past one. She's probably knitting you a sweater."

I wished.

Gladys' room was upstairs past the sewing room and at the other end of the hallway from the guest room I'd been given. Marilyn knocked on the door, and called softly, "Gladys. Gladys, are you awake?"

There was no answer.

She knocked again and called louder.

Still no response.

"She's not a heavy sleeper." Marilyn turned the doorknob and pushed the door gently open. "Gladys?"

Finally, she touched the switch by the door, and a table lamp came on. The room was empty. She looked at me quickly.

"Check the bath," I said. Gladys had her own large bathroom. I briefly wondered how many were in the house, as many as there were fireplaces? Again,

Marilyn called out for Gladys, and again there was no answer. She cautiously opened that door, too, and looked inside.

"Empty."

"Now the closet."

She looked at me oddly, but complied, not yet thinking in terms of foul play. The closet was a six-foot square walk–in in the northwest corner of the room. The fireplace butted up to it on the west wall, but the closet shared the north wall with the bathroom. It was only half-filled with clothes styled by an earlier generation and touchingly out of date. The floor was littered with boxes and suitcases that looked as if they'd been thrown in there. Not the type of disarray I'd have expected from Gladys.

"We should wake your aunts."

"Not yet. She may be downstairs in the library or the kitchen. There are a lot of places on the first floor we could look."

I followed Marilyn down the wide staircase, but doubted that we'd find Gladys reading a book or having milk and cookies.

Five minutes later, when it was clear Gladys wasn't on the first floor either, Marilyn suggested the basement, and we went down the final set of stairs.

It wasn't at all what I had anticipated in a house owned by two old women. This basement was designed for a family to live and play in. Marilyn told me that at one time, there had been playrooms for pool and ping–pong, a children's library, a cooled wine room, another room for a cook, and one for a maid.

This part of the house had been designed for a family to use, but years had passed it by, and now it was a hodge-podge of discarded and lost memories. Probably the only people to visit it in decades were the servicemen contracted to maintain the utilities.

"Gladys," Marilyn called out, tentatively. Again, no answer.

"If she's down here," I said gently, "It's for the police to find her. I think we should wake the others. Now."

Gloria and Judith were in a bit of a dither when we told them of the disappearance; they insisted on doing their own search, even extending it to the grounds and the garage.

Another hour passed before I could convince Judith to call the police. I didn't think it was necessary to tell them that we, Hobbes and I, feared that Gladys' disappearance came about because she had mentioned some pictures. I went to the sitting room to wait for them, and sat in the same chair I'd used some sixteen or seventeen hours earlier. I missed my sleep, and it made me grumpy, but I missed Gladys more. I was convinced that if we found her, we would find her too late.

About four o'clock that morning, the two cops, Al and Jack, came back to the house. It was their second visit that night. It could have been only the second visit by cops in forty years.

They looked at me suspiciously, but wrote a report and let me read it — Judith had provided the personal information about Gladys, and I learned her full name. A case for foul play looked pretty insubstantial, considering the séance and all. "Maybe," Al said, "she got an emergency call, and had to go somewhere."

"Ridiculous," was the firm answer from Judith. Gloria's feelings were hidden behind her veil.

"I'm sorry." Al closed his notebook and prepared to leave. "But she's only been missing a few hours. Except for putting out a general alert and hoping that she calls back here, there's nothing else we can do for now."

Judith glared at me as if the disappearance was my fault, which in part it might have been, and bade me an icy, "Good night, again." Then, she and Gloria went back to their rooms.

Marilyn and I sat alone in the quiet room, worry keeping her awake, and indecision doing the same for me. I needed to call Hobbes, but I wanted to use the house phone or the one in the car; I had no desire to take another walk. It wasn't like anyone in the house did not know that Gladys was missing. I opted for the car, if Marilyn would help.

"How?" she asked.

"Just let me back in when I knock. I want to make a call from my car." A very circumspect call. Almost five o'clock on Sunday morning and it was already getting light. I'd waited long enough.

Hobbes picked up the phone on the second ring. He must have been napping in his wheel chair, waiting. "Good morning, Chief." I said. "Have you slept well?"

"Well enough. And you?"

"Not enough. I need your advice. Gladys is missing. We don't have a criminal case yet, but I expect the worst. How do I proceed?" Translation: Nothing's going right. Should I get my equipment out of here before the cops ask for it?

For a moment, I could hear nothing but the squeaking of his wheelchair as he rocked back and forth.

Finally, he said, "Abel," and he sounded regretful, "If it becomes necessary for me to come up there, I should prefer to ride in the Town Car. Sally is in a hotel not far from you. I shall call her and ask that she check out, switch cars with you, and then come home, just in case I need to make the trip. Is that agreeable?"

"If she'll let me drive her Bronco."

He chuckled dryly. "She should be there in forty-five minutes."

Marilyn watched me carry my equipment from the library and stow it in the trunk of the Lincoln. She held the door open for me to reenter. Then, we waited until Sally honked at the gate.

Within thirty minutes after Sally left, I had taken a shower, brushed my teeth, pulled the shades down, and crawled into bed. The room was big and the bed adequate. Only the room needed vacuuming, I thought. There were black specks on the carpet near the fireplace. Another two minutes, and I was asleep.

This time, I dreamed of boxes and suitcases in a closet, and a rug that needed cleaning.

Six hours later, I woke myself up.

A Fine and Private Grave

I stared at the black specks on the carpet.

Chapter 11

My watch said twelve-thirty p.m., and my stomach growled, "Feed me." I took a quick shower, shaved, got dressed, and found my way downstairs to the kitchen. A subdued quintet acknowledged me without enthusiasm.

"We ordered some chicken. Nobody felt like cooking." Marilyn nodded toward the counter, "We have coffee and donuts. Cassius picked them up on his way over. Aunt Judith called him and Avery when she found Gladys was still missing." Her eyes were red and swollen — she seemed to accept the possibility that the worst had happened.

As for the others, well, Gloria wasn't wearing a veil, but she might as well have been; her eyes were focused on something far away. Judith's red hair was brushed back and hung loosely over her ears, but the cold blue gaze through her thick glasses was calculating and expectant. Avery still looked inconvenienced. I wondered if he would have come had Judith not insisted. Cassius seemed bewildered, whether by sadness or confusion, I couldn't tell. As I poured coffee and chose a glazed donut, I tried to decide who among the five was the best actor and the best liar. Undoubtedly, one of the group had chosen a dark and deadly path last night — one that passed right over Gladys.

"Were you entertained by the sitting, Mr. Houston?" There was no sarcasm in Judith's voice, just polite detachment. I couldn't judge her feelings about the disappearance, or even tell whether she was worried.

"Not exactly entertained," I tried a smile to see if my face was working yet. "Intrigued, yes."

"Then you have some questions. Ask them if you wish. We have nothing else to do except wait for news of Gladys."

"All right, Miss Borden. The candles and the fireplaces were managed well, and the physical atmosphere was manipulated as effectively as any I've seen. I give you an 'A' for effectiveness. But the knocking seemed contrived — anyone at the table could have done it. Why should I believe it was a ghost?" Actually, the individual control of seven candles so close together had been better than any I'd seen, anywhere. Not to mention the feeling of electricity, or the searching face in the candle's flame. Again, I wished Hobbes had been there.

"Did it sound like someone knocking on wood, Mr. Houston? Or like anything mechanical?"

"No," I admitted, "But we live in the age of the incredible. Because a knock sounds strange doesn't mean it came from another world."

"Of course not," she agreed. "And what did your incredible age recorders show you? Did they give any evidence of trickery?"

"We haven't checked them yet." I know I hadn't and I doubted if Hobbes had. He, too, needed sleep. Anyway, the nature of the case had changed —— from investigating the paranormal to investigating a disappearance that I believed would prove to be a murder. She leaned forward earnestly. "Whatever your machines show, remember this — Gloria is absolutely under the spirit's control through the entire sitting. It is the Eldred show, not the Gloria show."

"I'll keep that in mind. What did Gladys mean by water and clock?" I watched their faces, but of course, everyone had been expecting that question; if it meant anything to anyone, I couldn't tell.

"No one can answer that, Mr. Houston, unless Eldred chooses to."

"Do you have any idea who the 'someones' are?"

"No." Judith's eyes challenged me to believe otherwise.

At that moment, the phone rang. Cassius picked it up. "It's for you," he said. I walked around the table and took it in the relative privacy of the butler's pantry.

"Yes Chief," I said, thinking it would be Hobbes. I was wrong. It was my newest buddy.

"Abel, me lad!" The cheerfulness of Green's voice was the best thing I'd heard that early afternoon. "Me friends at the station house said two of their finest had been called a second time to the Bordens' residence. In the wee hours of this morning. I thought perhaps me good friend Abel had succumbed to another bit of trouble, and me not there to help him out." His Irish accent was straight out of some old Hollywood movie, and just as phony, but it made him seem curiously real. "Now I ask, do you need me assistance again?" I sensed a driving curiosity, and remembered his card —— *Ace Reporter*. Well, I owed him something from the night before.

"Yeah, Mr. Green, I do."

"Call me Forrest, me boy. Old friends should be on a first name basis, don't ye think?"

"Okay, Forrest," I said, though I wasn't sure I wanted to be on a first name basis just yet, "Yes, you could help me. But before I go any further, tell me, how did you know who I was, and why were you watching the Bordens' place?"

"Well, me bucko, it's a curious thing. The paper received an unsigned letter saying the Bordens were to engage Car'l Hobbes to investigate a murder. Well, you know the kind of paper the *Echo* is. The thought of a front page story about a murder, the Bordens, and Mr. Hobbes —— who is well known at the *Echo,* if not by the local constabulary —— made me editor weak in the knees. Not being weak in the head, he put me on it. I, being me, had no problem. Child's play it was to find out when they went to Hobbes' place in Meridian, and when you came here, and what you look like. A little watching of the entrance to this house, and a trifling bit of luck put me out front when you walked to *Toby's.*"

At best, his explanation seemed to leave a lot out, but it was probably as much as he could tell me without naming names.

"Uh-huh," I said. "Then you followed me into *Toby's* and pointed a box of Kleenex at me. What was in it anyway, a spy camera? No, not a camera —— a military surplus directional mic would make more sense."

He agreed. "A mic it was, me boy, with a recording device. But, it did me no good. You chose your phone well, being in a nice cozy noisy pub. Wiped out me mic, it did."

We shared a brief silence, and then he asked, "Do you have a question, me boy?"

"Yes," I said, "Forrest. How well do you know Tom Wilder?"

"Ah," he said, "Abel. I do know him, but not well. I might say he is two or three links ahead of me on the *Echo* food chain, but that's all. To speak more of him, I would have to know you better."

"Fair enough, but I would like to ask just one question. Did he send you here last night?"

"Me own editor sent me out, not the editor-in-chief, but little happens that Mr. Wilder doesn't know about. Now, other than that, is there naught I can do to help?"

"Could be, Forrest. There is something. It would put us pretty deep in your debt."

"I find that tantalizing, me boy. Would it be enough in debt to help get Mr. Wilder off the hook on a matter of some delicacy?"

Alarm bells went off in my head. Wilder and Hobbes were not friends, but they did know each other; Hobbes knew just how far he could trust Wilder. "I'll have to call my boss first before committing, but I'd say, probably yes."

"Then, look at page three of yesterday's *Echo*, me boy. That will tell you all you need to know. Now, you have me card, and you can call me when you have an answer."

"I'll do that," I said. The *Echo* was one of the dozen or so magazines and newspapers the Bordens had in their library.

"Then I bid you farewell," Forrest said.

Before I called Hobbes, I felt I should find out what Forrest thought was worth a trade, so I found my way to the Bordens' library.

If I'd been home and at Fred's breakfast table, I would have darnn near choked on my tapioca. I shouldn't have been surprised because it was the *National Echo* that I was looking at, a paper whose motto seemed to be, "*Any* news that's not fit to print," but, surprised I was. Even the *Echo* supposedly had its standards, however low they were. But this was in bold, black type, and took up a full quarter of page three. Whatever standards of respectability and taste the *Echo* once had were buried under the advertisement.

I read it again.

HEZEKIAH,

SHOW YOUR WORTH

PROVE YOUR GOD

TO US DISBELIEVERS

Be A Sacrifice

We Will do the Work

All you have to do is Show Up

SEE WHAT HAPPENS

Leave an answer in the bark of

the Medicine Oak at midnight.

We know where you live.

If you don't come to us,

WE WILL COME FOR YOU!

-signed-

The Witches of Meridian

The invitation was definitely not for a pleasant stroll in a park; I couldn't imagine any other newspaper running a quarter-page announcement like this. As editor-in-chief, Wilder had made *National Echo* the most successful tabloid in the Midwest, and kept it that way by staying on the leading edge of his type of journalism: always speculative, wild, and risky. But this was on the leading edge of idiocy. It was as if the paper was supporting human sacrifice. The risk of public outcry and accusation resulting from this particular ad was astronomical.

I went out to the car and called Hobbes. Again, for this call, security didn't seem very important.

My report took only a few minutes. Hobbes grunted about fifteen times as I repeated what was printed on page three of the newspaper. He asked me to have Green call him.

I called the make-believe Irishman and asked, "Would you mind telling Mr. Hobbes what you know?"

"Now, I'd be happy to." He sounded like he meant it; talking to the boss was probably what he wanted, anyway. They could help each other.

"He's expecting your call," I said.

"Thank ye, me boy. I'll ring him up now."

Back inside at the table, no one seemed to be interested in talking, but I tried anyway. I asked Cassius what he had done last night, after the sitting. He said he'd gone out back for a while and smoked a cigar. Then, he'd come into the library and had a whiskey or two before going home. Regasmun said he'd had a couple of martinis in the office at the back of the house, and had tried to catch up on some correspondence for the Bordens.

He always did that after a sitting, he said. That way, the evenings weren't complete losses. He'd gone home about a quarter after one, which was just before I got back. I remembered that Judith and Gloria had retired to their separate rooms shortly after the sitting, and presumably went to bed.

A few moments of silence hung in the air. Cassius picked at a crumb from a donut on his plate; I took a sip of coffee. When Gloria spoke, I almost choked. "Eldred has company. We would like to talk to Mr. Hobbes."

"Now, Gloria, my dear," Regasmun sounded uncomfortable. "Maybe we should wait till we hear something definite about Gladys before we have another sitting. Mr. Houston could go home and return later to continue his investigation."

"He's right, Gloria," Cassius said in surprising agreement with the lawyer. "If you continue now, you'll wear yourself out. A couple of days won't make any difference."

"No! We do not choose to wait. Mr. Houston, would it be possible for Mr. Hobbes to come this evening?" Apparently, the private meeting between Eldred and me would not happen on Monday and that annoyed me. I think I could have learned a lot, man to ghost, so to speak.

I grinned at the two men. "It appears she has the final word." I turned to Gloria. "I will call my boss right away. I'm sure he will come."

This call didn't seem to require a secure phone either, so I stepped back to the butler pantry and dialed.

"It's your nickel," Fireman Fred answered, which probably meant Hobbes was talking to Green; the phone had automatically switched to the kitchen.

"Is His Chairness there?"

"Naw, he's gone to church, ha, ha." Fred made a colorful telephone receptionist; Hobbes seldom turned on the answering machine. "He's on the porch, talking on the cordless. Hold on."

A moment later, I heard the familiar, "Yes, Abel."

"I'm calling from the Bordens' kitchen," I said. "Gladys is still missing. Gloria says Eldred has company and wants to talk to you. She would like for you to come for a sitting this evening. We're having fried chicken delivered for lunch; there may be some left over for supper."

For the next minute or so, all that came from Hobbes' end of the line was the New Orleans jazz station that he sometimes listened to. I didn't recognize the singer, but the song was "When the Saints Go Marching In". I thought there was a little irony there. Eldred, whatever else he had been doing, hadn't gone marching in.

Finally, Hobbes took a deep breath. "I had hoped to avoid a trip to Chicago. I suppose there is no way they could all come here."

"None, Chief. Do you want me to come home and drive you up here?" I asked that knowing he didn't like to drive in Chicago traffic. And he didn't like to be a passenger when Fred or Sally was being the chauffer. Fred at least was cautious and drove at a reasonable speed, but he was a white–knuckle driver. He did okay in the small town of Meridian, but when he was behind the wheel in the big city, he always seemed to be on the verge of panic; that annoyed Hobbes endlessly.

By contrast, Cemetery Sally drove her Bronco like she was on the Indianapolis speedway. She averaged two tickets a year and was continually under court supervision so she could keep her license. She deserved three times that many tickets if you went by the number of times she sweet–talked some gullible kind–hearted officer who said she was going a bit fast.

I was a bit surprised at Hobbes' answer: "No," he said. "I need you there for another purpose. I will have Fred drive. There is no need to save any chicken. We will eat on the way. Expect us there by seven. Is that all?"

"Tell Fred the Lincoln has a loose nut behind the wheel and that the tolls are going to cost seven dollars round trip."

"I'll make it a point. Anything else?"

"Yeah. Have there been any other calls from up this way?" Like from a guy in a green coat.

Chapter 12

"One call. He will come here and visit for a while this afternoon. You did well. There is no need for me to caution you again; you are aware of the danger in that house."

I agreed with him, said I'd continue to observe, wished him a safe trip, and started to hang up when he said, "One more thing, Abel."

"Uh oh," I said to myself; aloud I said, "Yes sir?"

"Sally has had very little success with the Bordens of forty years ago. The only newspaper to give serious attention to them was the *National Echo*. The *Echo* was also the only paper to refuse us access to its archives. Tom Wilder took special pains to refuse us, and frankly, Abel, I did not see any way to proceed with the investigation. Then, I saw that ad from the Witches of Meridian that you told me about. It occurred to me that Wilder had a problem too big to handle by himself, but of the kind that I have dealt with. Maybe we could make a trade –– my expertise for his files."

"Yeah," I agreed. "That's right up your alley, making a deal with Tom Wilder. Can you trust him?"

"Trust is irrelevant where he is concerned, but I have spoken to him on the telephone and given him my proposal. He has agreed to meet with you there at the Borden house at five-thirty this afternoon. Make him feel as unwelcome as you wish, but tell him Sally will wait in the lobby of the *Echo* only until seven p.m.

Tell him that I will arrive at the Bordens' by that time also, but that I will see him at eight." He hung up his phone.

A deal with Wilder? The two of them had been enemies for eighteen years; I think the last time they had spoken to each other had been from opposite sides of a courtroom. As Hobbes told Sally a few days ago, Wilder had been unhappy with the outcome, especially the part where the *National Echo* had had to pay Hobbes a hundred thousand dollars.

Someone paged from the gate, so Cassius excused himself. A few minutes later, he was back with chicken — baked, not fried — and several side dishes. I hadn't realized how hungry I was; I found my outlook much improved after I'd filled my stomach. I couldn't say the same for anyone else and finally quit asking questions, except for one.

"Would it be okay for me to look around outside?" The person I hoped would answer did so, and excusing ourselves, Marilyn and I went out the back door. She led me into the flower garden where we sat in a covered lawn swing, surrounded by a riot of colors and scents that I almost didn't notice. Her blue eyes met mine. Then suddenly, somehow we were holding hands and laughing.

"Do you really live here?" I asked. She seemed so alive — the house and those inside looked gray and lifeless in comparison.

"When I'm not away with my team — my research group. This year, I joined them in New Guinea for the first two months of summer break. They have spirit houses there, too." Her voice took on a dreamy quality and her eyes gazed at something far away. "At least in their primitive villages. Funny, isn't it? Primitive or advanced, society always demands spirits."

"Is that why you went into anthropology? To study spirits?"

"You mean because of Aunt Gloria? I've often thought so. She's sweet and innocent and totally unaffected by real life. Eldred's spirit, real or unreal, is all she relates to."

"I think she's more than that," I said, remembering her steely determination in front of Hobbes. "But tell me more about New Guinea." Just so I could hear her voice.

We got up and walked and talked the afternoon away. When we finally got tired of walking, we sat on a bench in back of the house and just talked, one of us mentioning a cruise on Lake Michigan and the other saying sure, after this job's finished. As I sat there thinking about putting my arm around her shoulder, I thought how beautiful everything looked, except for the house. There was something wrong with the house, or maybe just with its shape. Two chimneys — one from my room, one thirty or so feet to the east of Judith's — pierced the lower edge of the roof, but only the outer ends of the fireplaces could be located. Between them, the back of the house extended flush with the backs of the fireplaces.

For some reason, the arrangement looked wrong; I felt like I was missing some important detail. About then, Marilyn's soft red hair brushed against my face and I lost my train of thought.

Sometime later, Cassius came out the back door and paused, an odd expression on his face. I remembered that Marilyn was his daughter and gently disentangled myself. She looked at her father, then at me, and smiled. But she straightened up, too. "There's another newspaperman here to see you, Abel. He'll be in the library. And, food is on the table," he said dryly. "You may want to freshen up. Hobbes should be here in an hour and a half. We will begin the séance at seven." He turned and went back into the house. Where had the time gone?

"Cold chicken?" she asked.

"Go ahead, Marilyn. I'm overdue at the library."

Tom Wilder was waiting for me.

He slapped his hand on the polished oak of a library table and tried to grin at me when I walked in. "You've read the article, Austin? What do you think?" He looked trim and in good physical condition for a man of forty-five, but today a nervous tic in his right eye made him look older and not quite in control.

I started to remind Wilder that my name was Houston, not Austin, but let it go. He knew who I was well enough and had known for eighteen years. He just liked calling a person by the wrong name because sometimes, he had once said, it rattled a person who would then say something he hadn't intended to. He got better interviews that way.

"What do I think, Wilder? I think it's a bad joke. A stupid joke." I gave him time for a response, but his grin became a little tighter, a little thinner.

I held up the newspaper, opened to page three. "Is this a publicity stunt? Did you write it?"

"No." The corners of his mouth dropped. "Nor did I authorize anyone else to do it. I couldn't even keep it from the public because it was on the street for half a day before I knew about it. The waiter at a coffee shop showed it to me. It's a disaster for the paper! I did what I could to cut the damage. The next issue will have a half-page retraction and apology on the front page."

I asked the big question. "What do you want from Hobbes?"

"Look," he forced the word out. "Hobbes called me, not me him. He said he could take care of a little situation. That we could cut a deal. That I could talk to him here, tonight, but I had to talk to you first."

I knew exactly what Hobbes wanted. "Sally Wilson will be in the lobby of your *Echo* until seven o'clock. She wants the paper's complete file on the Borden family. She'll look it over, make notes as she sees fit, and then return it. If she gets what she needs, she'll call Hobbes. Then, he will take care of your little problem as soon as he can."

"You know I can't do that, Winston. Those files are confidential."

"They'll stay that way. Sally will wait until seven. It's a quarter to six now, so you will have to make up your mind soon. Hobbes will be here until at least eight; if Sally calls before then and says she has all she needs, then he'll talk to you right here in this library."

He stared at me for thirty seconds. "Just the files on the Bordens?"

"Just the Bordens."

"Okay Winston, Austin, Houston, whatever your name is. I'll have to go approve the access in person, but it's a deal."

He held out his hand, but I shook my head. "A handshake would be an expression of trust, and I trust only one of us."

He nodded and said, "Fair enough." and left to get his car.

Chapter 13

The electronic sentry let us know when Hobbes arrived at the gate; Cassius pressed a button to open it. I excused myself and met the car as Fred parked it in back of a Cadillac that probably belonged to Regasmun. Hobbes motioned for me to get in the back seat where I spent a few minutes bringing him and Fred up to date, especially about Wilder. I even described my dream.

Fred got the wheelchair and a pair of four-legged aluminum canes from the trunk. He held the wheelchair as Hobbes settled into it. For a moment, the boss surveyed the flower garden and the cars parked near it, then took two minutes to study the back of the house and the chimneys. I couldn't tell if he was offended by the architecture or not. His triangular face with its hooded eyes and drooping moustaches was inscrutable, as usual. Saying nothing, he wheeled to the back door and beckoned for his canes. With our help, he managed the five steps to the landing, and then waited as Fred brought up the wheelchair. He sat back down with a sigh, and we entered the back hallway.

As we passed by the kitchen, we saw Marilyn washing up some dishes. She turned and gave us a smile. "Gloria wanted to meet you in the spirit room. I think they're ready for you now."

Hobbes said, "Thank you, Miss Borden." We moved on toward the front of the house, but on the way, Hobbes took the time to peer into Avery's office to admire the paintings on the walls. He also stopped and studied the main stairway, then shook his head. Ignoring the library, he went directly to the spirit room.

He stopped inside the door and nodded to the three people already seated. "Judith, Avery, and you are Cassius, I presume?" Cassius nodded. Hobbes continued, "I regret that I couldn't come earlier, but I was engaged on your behalf; the delay was unavoidable. Abel has said that Eldred wishes to talk to me. Is that correct?"

"Gloria has said so, yes." Judith acknowledged. "She would like you to sit here." She pointed to the chair I had used the night before. "I will sit at your left. Mr. Houston will sit next to me, and Cassius will take Gladys' place. Avery, as always, will be next to Gloria. That will be six people and Eldred will make seven. We must ask your man to go to the sitting room."

Fred bowed slightly. "By yer leave," he said, and backed out. Hobbes used the table for support and moved from his wheels to the designated chair.

The opening routine was the same as the night before: the cooling of the room, the music, the dimming and quenching of all light, and the waiting. I could imagine Hobbes noticing the same things I had noticed, probably thinking the same thoughts. This time, nobody sobbed.

Gloria glided in and placed the candelabra in the middle of the table; again, Avery held the chair for her.

As before, the central candle flickered, quiet descended, and Gloria spoke. "Eldred, are you here?" The candle flared briefly. "Will you talk to us?" Two hesitant, faint taps answered her. "Do you know yet who murdered you?" A long moment passed without an answer.

"Eldred, do you know yet who murdered you?" she repeated. Finally, there was a faint tap, *No.* and, suddenly, unexpectedly a second tap, more firm and assertive than the first that changed the answer to *Yes.* In the shocked silence that followed, an anticlimactic third tap was heard. Three taps. Did that mean that now he wasn't sure?

Gloria continued in a voice that sounded timid and uncertain, "You have asked to talk to Car'l Hobbes?" Two quick taps. "Very well. Everyone, please place your hands on the table, and hold the hand of the person next to you."

Presently, we felt the electricity pass among us, and six candles went out. "Look at the light," she said. Once again, I saw the face in the flame of the single candle. It appeared to be searching. I wondered if Hobbes saw it, too. Then, the flame died. In the darkness, Gloria cried softly. I could hear people changing positions in their chairs. Someone — Cassius, I thought, cleared his throat. Wood in the fireplaces ignited as before. Gloria lowered her head as Eldred began speaking in that solemn, deep voice.

"Car'l Hobbes, we have been waiting for you."

"And I for you." Hobbes spoke as if he were really talking to the spirit of a dead man, and not to Gloria, although he had already called her a fraud.

"Do you know who we are?"

"Eldred Carpunky and Gloria Borden."

"Eldred and Gloria and one other. Now we are three."

"Who is the other?"

"You know who the other is."

Hobbes paused, thinking. "Why did you ask for me?"

"The other wants you to help."

"How?"

"Ask a specific. We can only answer."

Hobbes hesitated again. "Was the other murdered?"

"We don't know. The other was sitting and waiting and died."

"Did she... did the other have something she wanted to give me."

"The other had pictures."

"What did the pictures show?"

"Clock, water, a full moon. A house with cellar steps. Twins."

"Who killed Eldred?"

"We may know; we're not sure. We cannot point fingers. We cannot name a name. We ask you to do that."

"Where was the other when she died?"

"What is 'she'?" Eldred seemed to have trouble with certain pronouns, or maybe there was no gender on the other side.

Hobbes rephrased the question, "Where did the other die?"

The answer was slow in coming. "The other has said what the other must say. The other has moved on. Now we are two. Now one more must go."

"Wait," Hobbes said. But there was no answer. The lights slowly came back on.

He looked at Gloria, whose head had slumped to her chest, then looked slowly around the table. Avery had pushed his chair back and dropped his hands to his lap. Cassius was looking at me curiously, and Judith's face had turned very pale. No one was talking. Hobbes studied the candelabra with its seven candles; he picked it up and examined it more closely. The base with its seven points was dull black, as were the candles. He slid his fingers up and down the center one, and then replaced the candelabra on the table. He turned to Judith. "Are you all right, Miss Borden?"

"It's been a difficult day."

Cassius asked me quietly, "Figure it all out yet, Abel?"

"Not all of it," I admitted. "I don't know about Hobbes."

"Let me know when you do." He pushed himself up from his chair, nodded to us, and left the room.

"Mr. Regasmun," Hobbes said. "What about Eldred? Does he know who killed him?"

"Who is Eldred?" Avery Regasmun countered. "You talked to him. Is he real, or does he exist only in

Gloria's mind? Do you still think Gloria is a phony? Answer those questions first."

"She is unique in many ways, but I would not call her a phony –– at least not yet. When the investigation comes to an end, we may have to define a word that excludes self–deception."

Gloria seemed to return to normal –– at least she straightened up and looked around the room, settling on Hobbes. "Self–deception? No, Mr. Hobbes, I deceive no one, not even myself." She turned to her sister; "Judith, tell me what was said."

"There was another with you tonight. Eldred said you were three, but he wouldn't name the third."

"Three? Oh, no." Gloria put her hands to her temples and sighed deeply. "What was said? Tell me every word."

Regasmun scooted his chair back and stood up. "You tell her, Judith. I'm going to have a drink." Acknowledging the rest of us with a nod, he left the room. I heard the front door open and close, so I supposed he wasn't going to mix his own. On the other hand, his car was in back of the house, so, where was he going, *Toby's?* He didn't seem like a *Toby's* kind of guy, but you never know.

Judith took her time repeating the brief conversation between Hobbes and Eldred. I listened closely and was surprised at the accuracy of her account –– she even mimicked Hobbes' deep voice pretty well. I only noticed one mistake, or lapse. That was when Eldred had said, "A house with cellar steps. Twins." She had left out the word, "Twins." I didn't know if the omission was deliberate or accidental, but in either case I didn't see what difference it would make.

"Poor Gladys, poor dear Gladys," Gloria said.

I wish I could have seen her face, but her veil hid whatever emotion she felt.

"I believe I shall go to my room and lie down," she said softly. "Judith?"

"In a moment, my dear." Judith turned to Hobbes, "Is Gladys dead?" The question was flat, unemotional.

Before Hobbes answered, he made the transition back to his wheelchair and rolled over to the back fireplace. For a moment, he watched the fire consume the small logs. He drew a finger along one of the bricks just inside the fireplace, then motioned for me to come over. "Look," he said.

I stared at his finger for a long time, not surprised at what I saw. Soot. Black soot.

"If you find anything, call me after you call the police," he said too quietly for anyone but me to hear. "But wait an hour before you go upstairs. Allow me time to get home before the law knows I've been here." He returned to the table.

"Miss Borden," he said to Judith, "I cannot say whether Gladys still lives, but it is reasonable to assume the worst. If that is the case, then the police must be allowed to take charge, and I would prefer to not be here."

"Of course," Judith said. "Will you continue with your investigation?"

He nodded, "Yes, but from Meridian. Abel will stay here until staying has no further value, or until you send him on his way. While he is here, if you wish him to, he can be your liaison with the Chicago police. If, in fact, they do become involved.

"Now, unless you can think of something else I can assist you with, I'll be going home."

"We'll manage. Good evening, Mr. Hobbes," she said. She took Gloria's arm and the two of them walked toward the hallway and the stairs that led to their bedrooms.

"Chief," I said. "The library. Wilder."

"Sally has not yet called."

As if on cue, his cell phone rang.

He held it so I could hear, too. She spoke three words, "I've got it," and hung up.

Hobbes took a deep breath. "I can give him five minutes."

Neither man offered to shake hands in the library, but Wilder said, "Did she get what you wanted?"

"I think so," was the answer. "She has at least been given the files I asked for. I won't know if it is what will help until I see them. Unless there is some reason to have them back quickly, I would like to keep them for a few days."

"As long as you need them. Just be careful. When are you going to start work on my case?"

"I will begin as soon as I can. Right now, my firm is deep into a double murder investigation, and that must take precedence. If you could come to Meridian on Tuesday or Wednesday, that would help."

"You can't do anything tonight?"

"I will make a phone call when I return home. That will delay any further action on the part of the witches of Meridian."

The relief on Wilder's face was evident. "Then I'll call you Tuesday." A minute later he said, "Goodnight, Gracie," and left the building.

I followed my boss down the main hallway and through the one that led to the back of the house as he looked for Fred. We found him in the kitchen talking to Marilyn, drinking a glass of milk.

"Plenty of cold chicken left," I said. "Want some for the road?"

"I been eaten' it," he said to me. To Hobbes, he said, "Chief, you oughta try some."

"'For the road' sounds good, Fred. We should be leaving soon."

Marilyn took a box from the refrigerator and handed it to Fred, then offered her hand to Hobbes.

"Thank you and good night, Miss Borden," Hobbes said.

"Good night, Mr. Hobbes." She turned to Fred. "I didn't know there was so much to learn about fire fighting. We'll have to talk again."

"G'night, yerself," he said to her, his bald head reflecting the kitchen lights. "C'mon Abel, let's get the boss outta here."

We helped Hobbes down the steps; I followed him to the car where he again urged me to take care.

I had been waiting for him to tell me, but he hadn't, and so I had to ask. "Who are you going to call, Boss?"

"Why, no one, Abel," he said. "There is no one to call, but nothing will happen. That ad has served its purpose. We will have to wait to see what that is."

"Do you know who put that thing in the *Echo*?"

"We both know, Abel."

"Wilder?" I asked.

He didn't answer.

A moment later, he and Fred were gone. I glanced at my watch; it was barely nine. Wait an hour, he'd said. Well, it wouldn't make any difference to Gladys.

I went back to the kitchen, helped myself to a tall glass of ice water, and sat down by Marilyn. "Tell me more about New Guinea," I said.

At ten o'clock, I asked her if she'd come to my room with me. She looked at me very closely before answering. "This is nothing romantic, is it?"

"I wish it were."

She dipped her head in the most delightful way and murmured, "So do I."

Her words were most encouraging, but I thought it best to keep our focus on things less romantic. We took the stairs slowly and walked down the short hallway to my room. I went in first, not sensing any danger, but not knowing. Marilyn followed me.

Chapter 14

I showed her the black spots on the carpet. "I should have figured it out last night."

She frowned. "What are they?"

"Bits of soot, from the fireplace."

"But..."

"Then again, I could have caught on this afternoon when I saw how ugly the back of the house was. Did you know there's a hidden passageway between the fireplace in here, and the closet in Gladys' room?"

"Of course. We all do. It was for haunting special guests, and..." Her voice dropped off. "There's a secret door in the side of the fireplace."

"How do you open it?"

"You can't from in here. You have to go through Gladys' closet to get to the other side."

I tried to grin. "Sounds like something from an old horror movie."

"I think Aunt Judith had that in mind when she had a builder enclose the space between the two chimneys. That was twenty–five years ago, but I remember how upset Avery was when he came back from a business trip to New York and found the construction almost complete. He claimed it ruined the appearance of the back of the house, but I think the real reason he was angry was that she had done it without his knowledge."

"What did your Aunt Gloria think about it?"

"I'm not sure she even noticed it, Abe –– Abel. Does anyone ever call you Abe?"

"My friends did when I was growing up. Hardly anyone does now."

"Anyway, that was at the peak of their popularity, and Judith thought that a haunted room where special clients could spend the night would be a great success.

"You can probably visualize what she was thinking. Client goes into bedroom, bars the door, turns the lights out and crawls into bed. During the night he is visited by specters from the other side, although in this case, it's the other side of the door in the fireplace."

"Was it successful?"

"It never had a chance. When it was finished, Judith showed it to Gloria and explained her plans. Do you know what Gloria's reaction was, Abe? Abel, I mean."

"I can guess. And you can call me Abe. It sounds good the way you say it."

"She refused to be a part of anything that would commercialize her talent. She said she would not allow some horse-and-pony show to make this house into a circus."

I nodded. "There's a fine line between showmanship and perpetrating a hoax, isn't there?"

"And she wouldn't cross it. Judith was angry for a long time, but it didn't make any difference.

Avery wanted the contractors to put the house back the way it had been, but Aunt Judith refused to allow it. Too much money would have been wasted, she said, and besides, Gloria might change her mind someday."

"But she didn't."

Marilyn shook her head. "So, the secret passageway stayed, but as far as I know, nobody ever used it —— except for me and some friends when I was a kid. It was a great place to play. We'd close the doors from the inside and read Wonder Woman comics by flashlight. Sometimes, we'd be cavemen and paint pictures on the walls."

"But it's not a playroom anymore, is it?" I said. Playroom or not, I knew I'd have to see what was inside for myself, and I didn't much relish going into a narrow, confined space. I choked out the next words; my stomach was already knotting up. "I'll get my flashlight, go in, and get it over with."

I dug my Mini Maglite out of a suitcase, took a deep breath, walked out of my room, down the hall, and into Gladys' room. Marilyn was right beside me. That helped.

The room could have used half a dozen lights. As it was, only the lamps by the bed worked. They barely lit the closet door.

I did my damnedest to hide my shaking, but I couldn't keep my face from turning pale or stop the sweat from beading up on my forehead when I gripped the closet's doorknob.

Marilyn put a hand on my wrist. "Are you all right, Abe?"

I nodded and tried to smile. "A little claustrophobia. Let's get started."

I opened the door to the six-by-six walk–in closet, looked around for a light switch, found it, and turned it on. No light. The bulb must have been burned out. Not that it made much difference. The bedroom lighting provided enough illumination for the moment.

She still held my wrist. "Are you sure you're okay? You're trembling all over."

I took a few deep breaths. "I'm fine, Marilyn. Give me a minute."

"Why don't you stay here, Abe. I can go in and check things out."

"No," The word came out a little sharper than I'd intended, and I was immediately sorry. I was trying hard to stay under control. It would have been easy to step back and let her do it, but I had decided long ago that I would never let a little claustrophobia keep me from doing my job. I had let it keep me out of the astronaut program. That had been enough.

"You know what we're going to find?"

"Yes." Marilyn's face had turned pale, like mine.

We removed the suitcases and boxes from Gladys' closet, and slid the clothes out of the way. Even without interior lighting, I could see the small door near the outer wall and the slip bolt that held it closed.

"How wide is the passage? How tall?"

"Maybe two and a half feet wide, five feet tall."

"That's not enough room for both of us, Marilyn. I think you should go back to my room, and stay close to the telephone. I'll go through and open the door to the fireplace; you can meet me there."

"But..."

"No buts. If she's there, we don't want to disturb anything. So." I swallowed hard. "As a detective, I should be the one to go in."

"Okay," she said softly. "I'll be right there when you reach the other end. Yell for me if... if you need help."

I stepped into the closet and dropped to my hands and knees. I crept slowly but defiantly toward the small door in the back corner. Sweat ran down my back and dripped off my face, yet my skin had turned to ice. The passageway started a slow spin and I froze. I couldn't go on. Then, I thought of how I had let the claustrophobia keep me from my desire to go into space. I had given up too quickly. But never again.

I reached the door. I was suddenly that thirteen–year old kid, looking down into a manhole. I had to go in.

Sliding the bolt back and opening the door was easy. It was mounted so that it would swing itself shut, but I ignored that. Sticking my head in was hard. My guess, allowing for the width of the sewing room, was that the passageway was about fifteen feet long; I could see barely five of those feet. I twisted the barrel of the Maglite to turn it on. It gave me a dim yellow light for fifteen seconds, but then began to fade. Batteries. I'd forgotten to change them. I felt I was in a conspiracy of darkness, but I only needed two minutes. If I hurried, the light might hold out. I pointed it down the passageway; it reflected faintly off the slide bolt that held the door to the fireplace closed.

Something pale and shapeless lay on the floor next to the door. I raised my light as high as I could; whatever was down there shimmered in the distance. Well, I'd held off going in as long as I could, and my light was almost gone.

I sucked in a bushel of air, and held it as I counted to ten, then slowly let it out as I made my first step into the darkness. Brushing against the wall to my right, I began the long fifteen-foot walk. It wasn't all that bad. I'd been in worse places. At least there was a little light coming in from the closet, and my night vision was taking hold. I was six feet in when the door behind me gently swung shut. At the same time my flashlight died. The darkness became complete. I hugged the wall, crouched down as the ceiling began to fall. I reached out to the other wall to stop it from closing in and crushing me. Another deep breath, another ten count. The air was hot and filled with the stench of death. I wanted to run, but I'd lost all sense of direction. I wanted to sit down. I wanted to lie down. I wanted to hide so they couldn't find me.

I almost didn't hear the pounding of iron against brick, or the urgent call from Marilyn.

"Abe, Abel! Are you all right? Answer me! Are you okay?"

I could follow the voice. "I'm coming, I'm coming!" I stood and ran –– at least I thought I stood and ran, but it was taking an awful long time to cover that last ten feet.

I tripped on the thing that was on the floor and fell on top of it. It was bloated, full of gas, spongy. It was covered in plastic, but my hand found its face. I could feel the tongue sticking out, I imagined the eyes bulging. I rolled off of her and stood up. The banging was right behind me. I turned and felt the wall. I found the bolt, gripped it, and slid it back. The section of fireplace opened, and I stumbled out. Marilyn dropped the poker she'd been banging on the bricks with and caught me.

I said three words: "Call the cops." I stumbled to the bed and collapsed. Half a minute later, I got up and returned to the fireplace. I needed to report to Hobbes in detail, so I had to go back in and take a closer look. I waited another minute to allow my pulse to return to normal.

"Abe?" Marilyn took my hand. "You don't need to go back in there."

I withdrew my hand from hers and shook my head to clear the fog. The faint hint of her perfume seemed to help. "I have to."

The door on this end was smaller than the other one because it had to look like part of the fireplace, but it didn't matter. I still had to go back in. I knelt and peered inside, letting my eyes adjust to the warm darkness. A form gradually took shape. It was just a couple of feet away. I got on my hands and knees again and crawled toward it, my whole mind and body screaming to turn and run. But I moved forward. A plastic garment bag. Zipped tight. Something in it. I touched the bag. Moved my hand over it. Held my breath and unzipped it at the top. Studied the face, the eyes, the neck. Enough. I zipped it back up. Then, I backed out.

I stood up and Marilyn helped me to a chair. I breathed deeply, and waited for my pulse to slow down and the lump to leave my throat. Finally, I could speak.

"It's her."

She put her arms around me and cried.

Chapter 15

I wanted to go home. Back to the house on River Street. To a hot shower. To wash the sweat and the fear away. I wanted to bury my head under my pillow. To sleep. And then forget. But I'd dream. And I'd remember what happened that other time, when I was a kid, wouldn't I? At least, in my room on River Street, I could throw darts.

We called the police from the phone in Gladys' room, and told them we had found the body of the missing person, "Gladys Kelly Jones." That was the name Judith had given the detectives. Yes, she was dead. I was positive. No, we hadn't disturbed anything. Yes, we would wait for the authorities. A few questions later I was allowed to hang up.

"Your aunts will still be downstairs, won't they?" I finally asked. To my surprise, my watch said it was only fifteen past eleven, and it was still Sunday. We'd been employed for only two days.

Marilyn nodded. "Avery would be in the office, but I think Dad has gone home. We should prepare them, shouldn't we? At least the ones that are here?"

"Yes. I'll get Regasmun, and we'll meet in the library." I touched her hand. "Don't say anything till we get there. Okay?" I wanted to see their reactions.

"Okay."

We hurried downstairs, and I found the lawyer seated at his desk, a ledger open, and *Quicken* on his PC. He looked up at me with that familiar annoyed look.

"Mr. Regasmun, we have a situation. You and I have to meet the others in the library."

"I'll be there in ten minutes."

"No, sir. Now. What you're doing here can wait, believe me."

"Then I'll save this." He touched a key, and his machine chattered for a second. I saw his final entry go into computer limbo, and for an instant the screen saver — an unfamiliar moon surrounded by unblinking stars in the blackness of deep space — appeared, along with the logo of some financial institution, then it too was gone as he flicked the master switch. He stood up and growled, "Let's see your 'situation.'"

The library was one of the Bordens' more comfortable rooms, not too big –– about twelve by twelve –– but big enough for the bookshelves that covered most of the walls, and for two easy chairs, a leather sofa, and a study table with straight back chairs that gave the room a sense of purpose. I felt more at home there than in any other room, except maybe the kitchen. The sisters were already seated on the sofa; I motioned for Avery to join them.

"You look dreadful, Mr. Houston." Judith's remark seemed unnatural. Sympathy didn't fit her, somehow.

"And I'll probably look worse before morning. The police are coming."

"What in the world for?" asked Gloria. She sounded almost amused. I wondered how much of her mind was still connected to Eldred.

I watched them carefully as I said, "We found Gladys' body."

Gloria said, dreamily, "Eldred thought you would."

Avery's face turned deathly white. His eyes rolled upward, and his head dropped back against the sofa. The leather made a soft squeaking sound as he slipped downward. Marilyn caught him and bent him forward at the waist putting his head close to his knees. In a moment or so, he sat up, trembling.

Judith said, calmly, "Please excuse Avery. He doesn't handle bad news well. Where did you find her?"

"In the secret passage to the fireplace in my room."

"How did she die?"

"I couldn't tell. She was... wrapped in plastic." I decided it should be up to the police to give out the details.

"Oh, dear."

The gate pager sounded. The police were here.

I said, "They'll want to talk to you after they've been upstairs. You can stay here for now."

Judith said, "Thank you."

In less than ten minutes from the time of my call, and for the third time in two nights, officers Al and Jack — their nameplates said McDivitt and Hart — came to the Bordens' home. Marilyn and I let them in.

Al greeted me, a wry smile screwing up his face. "So, Cuz, I guess it's for real this time."

"Yeah," I said. "For real."

He brushed his hand across his holster. "Lead the way." The two cops followed us upstairs into Gladys' room.

I showed them the closet. "It leads into a secret passage to the next room. The body's in there."

Jack dropped down and peered inside. "I'll go look," he said, and crawled through the small doorway, a flashlight in his hand. We heard the distant rustling of plastic, and a low whistle. A few minutes later, he reappeared. "Hot in there," he said, "And it's starting to stink already. Belly's blown up like a watermelon." He stood and stretched, not bothered by the closeness of the passage. "Better get CID out here; nothing accidental about this."

"Make the call, Jack," Al said. Then he turned to me. "Okay, Cousin, how'd you find her?"

I took him to my room and pointed out the soot spots on the carpet. "There's a secret door in the fireplace that opens from the inside."

"And you think she was killed in here?"

He asked a lot of questions, and I answered them carefully, knowing that the detectives from homicide would ask me the same questions later.

I was painfully aware that our original objective of exposing a supernatural hoax had changed to exposing a cold-blooded murderer, and that the answer to one could well be part of the answer to the other.

Shortly after midnight, I was introduced to a giant, or so he seemed — Kyle Murphy, homicide detective. Close-cut red hair nearly touched the top of the doorway his frame tried to fill; he entered the bedroom like a bull, graceless and intimidating. He looked down at my six feet as if I were a reptile crossing his road and he was undecided whether to slow down or just run over me. "You got a private eye license, huh? Lemme see it."

I started to reach inside my jacket, but he grabbed my wrist and twisted it up and away. "Better have a license for that, too, Buddy." With his other hand, he lifted my pistol from its holster and tossed it on the bed. He had caught me by surprise and his grip was intense and painful. I looked up at him, anger and a rush of adrenaline giving me power. Ever since I was fourteen, I'd worked hard to build strength and stamina. I had dreamed it would help me get into the Program, but even after I washed out, I kept up with the workouts. I suppose bitterness and a feeling of betrayal, and maybe a faint hope, kept me working at it. You never knew when you might get a second chance.

I had never built up a lot of mass, but my muscles were stronger than most and my size was misleading. So, without putting out a lot of visible effort, I brought my hand back down slowly, matching his bull's strength with my own. His eyes widened in surprise as his hand unwillingly followed mine. His hand was still holding my wrist as I reached inside my jacket and pulled out my leather case.

He glanced around quickly and, since nobody seemed to notice our brief exchange, released me. For a few seconds he stared at his hand, as if it had turned on him, then he locked eyes with me. I flipped my case open, but he didn't look at it. "Keep one thing in mind, little man," he said, lowering his voice. "There are two laws in this town: Chicago's, and Murphy's. And right now, you're in Murpheysville. Get it?"

"I don't care where we are," I said, under control again. "Find out who killed her. I'm willing to help if I can."

"Damn right you will," he muttered. "As soon as I ask for it." And that, I thought, would be about the time hell started cooling off. "Wait here." He turned and walked over to the fireplace. Other officers had just opened the secret door from the inside. I went to a corner out of the way, turned a chair backward and straddled it, my arms resting on the high back. I watched the circus.

There are good men here, I thought, good forensic detectives. The problem was, the wrong man was in charge.

Two men in white jackets began gently pulling the body — still wrapped in plastic — through the fireplace when Murphy said, "I'll get that," and muscled his way in between them. He grabbed the top of the bag and pulled hard. It came out quickly all right, but the bottom of the bag's zipper caught on the door latch; the bag split up the middle. Gladys' upper body was suddenly exposed. Even before Murphy stepped between me and the body, I saw her swollen purple tongue, and bulging, accusing eyes. I also saw what she'd been strangled with, and swore to myself that I would find her killer.

Murphy growled over his shoulder, "Get him out of here." I walked to the bed, picked up my gun and stuck it in its holster, and then walked out of the room without looking at the Lieutenant. The room was beginning to smell anyway. She'd been stuck in that hole for twenty-four hours, dead, in the August heat. Her flesh would have started putrefying as soon as the sun warmed the unventilated passage. How long would it have been before the stink would have become noticeable in the bedroom? Three or four days? A week? Both doors to the passage seemed to have been pretty well airtight. Still, if the killer did not want her body found, he or she would have needed to move the body soon, but that would have been impossible while I was still in the house. I grimly recalled that both men had wanted me to leave — and for all I knew, so did Judith.

I was suddenly hungry. I visited the kitchen and helped myself to a cold chicken leg, which I ate there, and a can of Coke. Then, I returned to the library.

Gloria lay on the sofa, sleeping, while Judith and Avery sat on the easy chairs, listening to music from an old Zenith console stereo. Marilyn was on the floor leaning against the sofa. She smiled at me as I sat down beside her; I took her hand.

"Anything to report?" she asked.

"Yeah. Murphy's Law."

She looked puzzled. "Isn't that supposed to be, 'If anything can go wrong, it will?'"

"'And, at the worst possible moment,'" I added. "Wait. You'll see what I mean."

"I don't understand."

"It means that any real evidence up there will probably be destroyed. I should have looked everything over thoroughly before I called the cops." Sure, I thought. Just crawl back in there and look.

"Couldn't that have cost you your license?"

"Only if I were caught." There were worse things.

We made small talk for half an hour and watched Judith drift off to sleep, while Avery stared at something far away in space. Finally, the door opened and Murphy stepped in. He paused and looked around, gazing down at Marilyn and me for a long second, until we both stood up.

"The old folks can go to bed," he said loudly, his voice subdued by the hundreds of books, but still strong enough to wake Judith and Gloria. Avery glared at him, but mentioned that there was a day bed in the office where he could sleep. He waited for Gloria, holding the door open as she seemed to glide from the room. Judith's icy gaze might have frozen a lesser man, but the big detective ignored her. With deliberate slowness, she turned off the stereo, and then she, too, left.

"McDivitt told me what's been going on, and I didn't see any reason to keep those old people up any longer. They're not in the picture anyway, as I see 'em. An old witch, a quack fortune teller, and a shyster. Not one of 'em strong enough to move a dead body." He looked around the room. "Be a nice place for a pool table, you get rid of the books."

I had to squeeze Marilyn's hand hard several times to keep her quiet. "Who is in the picture?" I asked. In one sentence, he'd eliminated two of my three possibilities, although I disagreed about the strength of Gloria and Judith. I had felt their iron grips. Besides, Gladys had been skinny and frail. She might not have weighed ninety pounds.

"Her and you," he said, meaning Marilyn and me. An expression of cunning crossed his face as he gazed at Marilyn, "And your dad, Cassius." If he expected a reaction from her, he was disappointed. She met his eyes in stony silence.

Finally his face relaxed a little. "Ah, hell," he said, letting out his breath. "It's too late at night, or too early in the morning for games. Sorry. You two sit. I want to ask some questions." He brought over one of the chairs from the table and sat down, facing us.

His bully's facade disappeared, and for a split second, I wondered if it had been an act. Then, I remembered the body falling out of the plastic, and the way he had twisted my hand. Act or not, there was a mean spirit inside him.

"Houston, you saw that soot on the carpet yesterday. Why did you take so long to figure out she was in back of the fireplace?"

"I didn't know about the secret passage until last evening." But I'd had clues. Judith had talked about six fireplaces, and about hidden doors. I just hadn't put them together.

"What do you think she was doing in your bedroom?"

"Waiting for me. I think she had some pictures."

Chapter 16

"Pictures of what?"

"I don't know. They could have been more than forty years old."

"She got herself killed for some forty-year old pictures?"

"Yeah. She was going to show them to me when she found them. I imagine she came to my room through the passageway and I wasn't there, so she decided to wait. She moved a chair into the middle of the room and sat there facing the door — the soot on the carpet indicates that location. If she'd turned the chair any other way, she'd have seen the killer come from the fireplace. Or maybe, she fell asleep. Who knows? Whoever came out of that passage probably brought a murder weapon along, but decided not to use it. The irony of sending Gladys into another world using something on the bed was probably too good to pass up — so the killer took it, slipped it around her neck, and strangled her."

"So Gladys waited for you?"

I sighed. "Waited too long. I was delayed."

"Yeah," he growled. "By an hour and a half on the phone at Toby's Bar. The cops did the right thing stopping you, you know."

"Sure," I agreed flatly. I may or may not have been back in time to save her, but I would always wonder. "And I'd have ended up downtown getting my picture taken, if it hadn't been for the reporter."

Murphy's brow darkened; his neck turned fiery. "That phony little Irish bastard. If he butts in while I'm here, I'm going to grind his phony little head into one of those damn fireplaces!"

So, the *Echo's* ace had gotten to him. It would be worth going out of my way to hear that story. I could grow very fond of Forrest Green.

"How about that crippled egghead you work for? Why'd he leave so quick last night?"

"You'll have to ask him."

"Yeah. When you came here Saturday, you brought a bunch of cameras. What happened to them"

"We used them for the séance Saturday and sent them home Sunday morning. It wasn't evidence. According to the police, no crime had been committed yet. Ask Al and Jack."

"Yeah, the séance. Fat lot of help that would be." He turned again to Marilyn. "What did you do after the thing ended, until Romeo here woke you up at one-thirty?"

"I sat in here and read for a while. Then I went to bed."

"Were you by yourself?"

"I always sleep alone, Detective Murphy."

"I mean here."

"Yes, but I left before my father came back."

"And Regasmun was in his office, both the old ladies were in their own bedrooms, and your old man was out smoking a cigar. At least until you went upstairs. Well, well, well." He gave me a sour smile.

"No one has an alibi except for you, Houston. By the way, you'll have to find some other place to sleep. We're going to seal off both bedrooms."

I glanced at Marilyn.

"There is a very comfortable couch in the sitting room," she said in a *very* neutral voice.

Sounds from the hallway told us the coroner's people were leaving; taking with them what was left of Gladys.

One of the men in white came in and motioned to Murphy. The detective shook his head. "I'm busy; you want something, you say it out loud."

The man shrugged. "You're the boss," he said. "You know those pictures we found in the bag with the body? They've disappeared."

Murphy's face went from red to white. "They damn well better be where I left them!" Forgetting Marilyn and me, and rushed out the door, shoving the technician aside. We could hear his footsteps thundering up the stairs.

"Where'd he leave the pictures?" I asked the tech.

"On the table outside Miss Jones' room."

"Unguarded?"

"Who needs to guard anything with *him* around?" The question was academic. "Ask him. He's got the answer for everything." He was apparently surprised by his reckless comment about his boss. As he turned to leave, he added, "Forget I said that."

A few minutes later, Murphy and some unfortunate subordinate he was chewing on came back down stairs and went out the front door.

Shortly after that, Officer Al McDivitt came into the library. "It looks like we're finished for now, but there will be more people here tomorrow. You folks might as well get some sleep."

"Before you leave," I said, "tell me something. What charm school did they get him out of?"

"Murphy? He came with local politicians. His uncle is CEO of Triton Trust and Savings. Uncle Bradley Murphy bought and paid his nephew's way in and up the ranks. Some say Bradley has almost as much political clout as the mayor." The policeman was philosophical about it. "But don't worry. He won't be back tomorrow. It will take him at least one day to write his report so that everyone else looks incompetent."

He paused at the door. "Don't take this too personal, Cuz, but if we meet again, I hope it's in the daytime. After midnight, you've been nothing but bad news times three." He gave us an off-hand wave and was gone.

I had no doubt the pictures were gone, too.

I needed to talk to Hobbes.

My watch said it was Monday, four a.m. I'd worked the midnight shift for two nights with only six hours sleep in between. I really did need to call the boss, but the outer parts of my brain were starting to feel fuzzy. Anyway, he probably had some pretty good idea about what had happened already. He wouldn't have known about the pictures, of course, but bad news like that could wait. And I'd need to find another safe phone. That, too, could wait.

Marilyn agreed that business should wait and got a pillow and some blankets for the oversized couch in the sitting room. As she went around the room closing the blinds, she talked quietly. "Abe, when we first met, you called yourself a paranormal snoop. Was that a slip of the subconscious? I mean, if I took the phrase literally, I'd think you were an embodied spirit from the other side who was snooping around in the real world. I know Hobbes is a skeptic about everything, but what about you? Do you believe in the paranormal or in the supernatural?"

I kicked off my shoes and fell back on the couch. "I don't really know, Marilyn. Sometimes I think so. But the ghost of Eldred possessing Gloria?" I shook my head. "No. I think this situation is more psychological than ectoplasmic. There might or might not have been a murder forty years ago, but someone believed Eldred — or Gloria — enough to consider Gladys some kind of threat and killed her because of it. Her murder was real enough." I let Marilyn spread a blanket over me. "But I could be wrong about Gloria. I've been wrong before."

"Do you have any idea who the killer is?" I supposed it was her way of asking, *Which one of us do you think did it?*

"I don't know yet," I said, and closed my eyes. "I'll let Car'l Hobbes figure it out."

She leaned down and kissed me. "What's the apostrophe for?" is what I think she said, but I was already fading out. In a minute, I was asleep. What I dreamed about was my business.

Westminster chimes from the hall clock wakened me. Funny, I hadn't heard them during the séances. They would have been distracting. Someone must shut them off for the sittings, I supposed. Anyway, it chimed eleven times.

I used the bathroom downstairs to shower and shave, but I had to get dressed in the same clothes I'd slept in. Murphy had been true to his word and both bedrooms were sealed — technically at least. Half a dozen or so men were going over the crime scene picking up where the night crew had left off.

Breakfast was fresh coffee and stale donuts left over from yesterday. Apparently no one as yet was ready to take over Gladys' job as cook. I was working on my second cup — no donuts — when I heard the back door open.

Cassius stuck his head into the kitchen, and seeing only me, went to the counter and poured himself some coffee. "Morning, Abel," he said quietly. "Or is it 'mourning?' It's a damn shame. She didn't deserve that." He looked me in the eye, daring me to doubt his sincerity. "It had to be someone in the house who killed her, didn't it? Five suspects, not counting you?"

Regasmun stopped at the door to his office, across the hall from the kitchen, gave me a sour look, and then went inside and closed the door partway.

"He gets my vote." Cassius said.

It was the first accusation I'd heard from anyone. "Avery?" I tried to sound surprised. "Why Avery?"

"Why not? It's either him or me, or my daughter, or Judith. It wasn't me. Couldn't be Gloria. She's an original innocent. He's been hanging around the sisters for sixty years. Ask him why."

"Why? Why?" Regasmun barged out of his office, voice trembling, face livid. "What do you know about anything? About life? About responsibility? I'll tell you why I've stayed with her! I've stayed because I love her. I've loved her since before you were born. I'd have traded my soul for the return of that love." His color changed from red to white, and he put his hand on the doorjamb for support. "If I were your age, and your size, I'd teach you some *respect!*" He glared at us one more time, and then turned back to his office. He hadn't said which sister was the one he had loved.

Cassius looked at me and shrugged, "I'll make you a deal. You decide to nail him and I'll give you all the dirt you need."

"For murder? If you can tie him to Gladys' death, you should tell the police."

"For other things," he said.

"I'll mention it to Hobbes." My stomach growled suddenly. "Where can I go for a good breakfast?" He told me that there was a strip mall north on Halstead that had a *Denny's*. I thanked him, and asked him to tell everyone, including the police, if they should wonder, where I was. He said the sun was hot and very bright, and maybe I'd like to borrow a cap from one of the pegs by the back door. Vindictive one minute and considerate the next. He was a puzzle I couldn't put together. I took a red and black *Chicago Bulls* cap, the only one there.

Sally's Bronco was not my idea of a city car, but she'd always said it could take you anywhere, country or city. It took me to Denny's. I wondered if she had come back to Chicago; was she driving the Lincoln, which she thought of as a tank?

I hadn't really eaten a decent meal since I left home, orange roughy and calamari included, and I tried to make up for it with a skillet breakfast, a waffle, and two coffees. There's nothing like home cooking, and this was nothing like Fred's home cooking.

Most of the stores in the mall had outside entrances, but a few of them shared a two-story lobby that boasted three pay telephones and one stool. I snagged the stool, positioned myself with my back to a wall, spun the *Bulls* cap around to put the bill in back so I could see the second floor, and called collect.

"Good afternoon, Abel."

"Good afternoon, Chief. I'm ready to make my report."

"The recorder is on, Abel."

"Right." I told him about the entrance through Gladys' closet and the passageway to my fireplace. I minimized the part about my crawling to the body, but he understood, and told me so. I continued the narrative with the arrival of the police and gave my personal opinion of Lieutenant Murphy. At one point I asked, "Care to guess what she was strangled with?"

"It must have been something of significance, to judge by your voice."

"More of a personal nature."

"Well?"

"A silk tie with the NASA emblem painted on it."

There was silence for a moment.

"Could there have been two such ties in that house?"

"Not likely."

"Very well." There was a razor sharpness to his voice that hadn't been there before. He had given me that tie after I'd worked with him for five years. At the time, it had been a special gift, part of a victory celebration. I considered it a sort of good luck charm and took it with me when I went traveling, but I never wore it –– almost never. Its use as an instrument of death had made the murder personal for him as well as for me. "Continue."

"It gets better," I said, and told him about Murphy and the lost pictures.

"No matter. There will be other trails that the cretin hasn't trampled down."

I finished my report, and he did his usual cross-examination. Then I asked my questions.

"Has Sally had any success up here?"

"Remarkably little. She found some history of the Bordens from 1957 until the present, nothing spectacular. They have apparently lived a life quiet and above reproach. Regasmun retired from a small law firm fifteen years ago. It has since faded into obscurity without leaving any records behind. Sally is very disappointed and depressed."

"Have you had a chance to study the videos and tapes?"

"Yes, with some satisfaction. It may be helpful for you to examine them when you come home."

"What do you think of Forrest Green?"

"He is a man of dubious ethnic background, Abel. Nevertheless I believe he is a man we can trust. We have entered into an informal agreement. He will assist Sally as she goes once again to search the archives of the *National Echo* for information about the Borden family. In turn, we shall give him an exclusive story. When the case is concluded. Sally is in their Loop offices right now. She has been there since ten o'clock this morning."

"I thought she took the Borden files yesterday."

"What she had was nothing but fluff. Wilder had apparently sorted them before Sally got there." Hobbes didn't seem disturbed by the treachery. Maybe it was what he expected.

Chapter 17

"Just a minute," I said as I saw an unpleasantly familiar hulk come in the main door and look my way. "I'll call you later. The ugly hand of the law is here." I hung up the phone.

Murphy strode over and glared down at me. I didn't stand up. No respect for the law, not for this law, anyway.

"Who said you could leave the house, Houston?"

"You did."

I could see him work that over for a second. "The hell I did."

"Implied permission. You didn't say I couldn't leave. Matter of fact, you didn't even say good night."

He started to grab the front of my shirt, but thought better of it. His hand dropped to his side. "Listen, little man, I want you back there. Now. This is a damned murder investigation."

"Cool," I said. "Then you found the pictures."

His face turned red. "There weren't any damn pictures. There's nothing in my report about pictures. I want you out of here and back there. *Now!*"

I stayed seated. I wished I'd had a cigarette to light for the dramatic pause, but I didn't, so I simply said, "Murphy, you're suppressing evidence. What will Internal Affairs say?"

"What?" His fists clenched and unclenched at his sides.

"They could subpoena the men who were there last night. What do you suppose they'd say? Do you think they're loyal enough to lie for you?" I lowered my voice. "Not that I.A. really has to know. I'll make a deal with you. You go about your business and let me go about mine, and the pictures will stay a secret as far as Hobbes and I are concerned. With all of us free to investigate, maybe one of us will find out who killed Gladys."

I had to give Murphy a little credit. He knew when he was beat. After the barest hesitation, he held out his hand and said, "Deal."

I reluctantly shook his hand as we tested each other's grip. It was as close to civil as we were ever likely to come with each other. As he walked away, it occurred to me to wonder why he had personally come here looking for me. He could have sent someone. And then he had given in rather easily. Why? Had he thought that we might cause him trouble because of the lost pictures? Or was my offer to trade silence for freedom exactly what he'd come here hoping to get? If it was, then I had underestimated him. He bore watching.

On my way back to the car, I glanced at the display in a bookstore window and stopped to read a title. Exactly what Hobbes needed, I decided. Ten minutes later, the book and I were crossing the parking lot, heading for the Bronco. I must have been anticipating his reaction too much because I barely noticed a car slow down about twenty feet away, nor did I think anything when the passenger's darkened window went down.

I did hear a muffled *pop* and saw a small hole appear magically about three feet ahead of me, in the side glass of a camper. A second pop and a hole six inches away from the first brought me back to reality. I dropped to the asphalt, trying to reach my holster. The *pang* of the third bullet penetrating metal was followed by the squealing of tires as the car raced away. I stood up cautiously, much too late to see more than the tail end of the car as it disappeared around the *Denny's* where I'd eaten lunch. I checked the camper. The third bullet had penetrated just a few inches below the holes in the glass. They formed a good tight pattern — had a sharpshooter missed me on purpose? I took a breath to still the thudding of my heart while I looked around the parking lot and considered. No one seemed to have noticed anything. Which wasn't a huge surprise, since the gunman had used a silencer. Was this a warning? Someone hired to scare me off? I could hardly believe that.

I rubbed a hand across my forehead and realized I still had the cap on backwards. A red and black cap, on backwards. Were they the colors and symbol of some gang and I was on their turf? I took it off and stuffed it into the bag with the book. Should I call Hobbes? One of our unwritten rules about gunfire said yes, so I headed back to the telephone. I should have called the cops, too, but I couldn't see any immediate need. I did wonder what the owner of the camper would think when he found the bullet holes, so I took the time to memorize the license number for Hobbes. If the boss wanted to contact the owner some way to ease the man's mind, he could.

A few minutes later, Hobbes asked when I'd return home. "Probably tomorrow," I answered. "I want to ask one of the detectives at the house about those colors to see if the warning could be gang related." I also had another and better reason for not rushing back.

"And if they are gang colors, you may feel secure and let your guard down. Don't do that. Treat it as a genuine threat from the murderer. I have warned about the possibility of personal danger, Abel. If anything, the danger has increased. Keep your eyes open. Watch your back."

"Right," I said. The bullet holes were real enough.

"Get the details of the funeral, too, Abel. I wish to pay my respects."

Nothing else happened on the way back to the Bordens'.

The police had apparently completed their investigation. They were packing up equipment, preparing to leave as I arrived.

One of the technicians came over to me. "You can get your stuff out of there now — the rooms aren't sealed anymore," he said. "Murphy called and told us to cooperate with you. He sounded pretty cheerful, like he'd just put something over on someone." He grinned, sort of man-to-man. "If I was that someone, I'd be watching my back."

I asked if he knew about gang colors, especially red and black. He looked at me curiously, but said they sounded familiar. He also mentioned that I was free to leave anytime. Murphy had decreed it.

It was a little after four p.m., and I wondered where Marilyn was. Her Mercedes hadn't been parked in the circle drive when I left, or when I returned. The sisters were in the library, and Judith supposed that Marilyn had gone to the university.

I tried to make some conversation with Judith. I asked if either she or Gloria had ever been married, or come close to it.

"One of us almost married, once upon a time, but it wasn't to be. The man was fickle and irresponsible. He disappeared."

"Was his name Eldred?" The question was asked almost before I had time to think it.

She was slow to answer, "I don't recall. It may have been."

I turned to Gloria, who was holding a book in her lap. "Was it?" I asked.

She closed the book gently and looked at me through blue eyes rimmed with tears. She nodded.

Judith squeezed Gloria's hand and glared at me. "I can tell you this much. After that man left, we took an oath that there would never be another. I would allow no man to touch the heart of Gloria, and she would in like manner protect me."

There didn't seem to be much else to say, so I picked out a book on anthropology and went to the sitting room to read.

Marilyn came home about seven p.m. Her face was pale and her eyes puffy, but she seemed to have gotten past most of her grief.

"I went to the university," she said. "We've been working on an exhibit of primitive man and how they handled loss of a family member. I don't think modern man does any better. You'll have to come and see it someday."

I squeezed her hand and asked if she was hungry.

"Starved," she said.

Marilyn and I went to *Toby's* for supper. We ate ribs and talked and drank beer. At ten, though, we called it a night and walked back home. By eleven, I had brushed my teeth and made my bed on the couch for the second night — the guest room would have been haunted by the ghost of poor Gladys, figuratively speaking.

Before I allowed myself to sleep, I went over the day's events. It surprised me to realize that the gunshots didn't seem to be very significant. Rather, the *deals* were what felt important: Regasmun saying he'd have traded his soul for Gloria's love, Cassius offering a deal to nail Regasmun, Hobbes making an agreement with Green, me trading knowledge of Murphy's bungling for freedom to investigate, and Judith and Gloria swearing to protect each other from men.

Should one of those deals be telling me something? Telling me who the killer was?

I thought about it for the allotted two minutes.

Chapter 18

Tuesday morning, Tom Wilder called and we made an appointment for nine o'clock Wednesday morning. Nothing was said about the Borden files.

Tuesday morning, the *National Echo* printed a front page retraction and apology. An editorial on page two said the *Echo* would do whatever it took to find out who was responsible for that appalling article. It mentioned the hiring of a well-known private investigator.

Tuesday morning, the coroner gave a preliminary report about Gladys' death. It said that she had been strangled and labeled her death a homicide. The report concluded that she was killed by person or persons unknown, possibly by an intruder intent on robbery.

Also on Tuesday morning, the coroner's office released the body to Regasmun as there was no known next of kin. A funeral director came at his request and, I suppose, took care of all the details. The wake was to be Thursday evening; a private funeral would be held Friday, with just the Bordens and Regasmun attending. No one said whether there would be graveside rites.

Marilyn told me later that she had talked to the coroner. As far as the murder investigation went, he had said, the police weren't having any immediate success.

That hadn't stopped Lieutenant Murphy from voicing his own conclusions. He began insisting that an unknown intruder was responsible. He said that Gladys had walked in on what was most likely a burglary in progress, and it had cost her her life. I wondered if the coroner had agreed, but Marilyn told me he did not. He said the facts didn't fit. She speculated that he had given in to get Murphy off his back. She also speculated that they were all eager to just wrap this up since Gladys was not a person of any importance in their estimation Marilyn wasn't happy about the situation, but I told her to wait and see what Hobbes was able to do.

For the time being, we were all free to go about our everyday activities, just so we stayed where we could be found if Murphy needed us.

Marilyn said she should go to the university, and would probably be busy the rest of today and all of tomorrow. I decided it was time to go home, so I loaded my things into the Bronco and headed west.

I parked in back of the house on the cement pad next to the garage, slipped Hobbes' book under my arm, and walked around front to see how Clyde Butler, Richie's dad, was doing with the painting. A short man, balding, and facing middle age, he seemed unable to slow down. Even as we talked, he cleaned the nozzle on his spray gun.

"Decided to use some of my vacation for this," he said, grinning. "Hobbes don't know it yet, but he's gonna pay for the family's trip to the Ozarks." He had been giving the stucco a fresh coat of white paint. "Got a lot of work to do around those bay windows, but Richie's helping me. He's been doing a man's work, scraping and masking."

"Looks like a job for three or four men," I said. The front of the house was the worst. The previous owners had added a roofed porch to the first floor that ran the width of the building. Supporting columns and rails made the house look massive and substantial, but greatly increased the amount of trim to be prepared and painted. The wheelchair ramp that used half of the six-foot width of the steps was the only thing that looked out of place. Hobbes had required its installation before he moved in.

Clyde laughed. "You ain't seen the Butler team at work. We'll be finished with the outside by Friday night, and do the inside Saturday."

"Inside?" I'd forgotten about the boss' plan to remodel part of the basement.

"That's right. Mr. Hobbes said he'd be talking to you about it today."

Basement. Sure. That reminded me of the cellar steps that Eldred had spoken of so mysteriously, and I figured it was time to talk to the boss.

Clyde went back to painting, and I went in the front door, down the hallway, and turned right. Hobbes was entertaining a visitor.

A young man with sun-bleached hair and an open, friendly smile, nodded at me. His dark gray suit and tie suggested some branch of the government.

Hobbes spoke first, "It's good to have you home, Abel. Did you have a restful holiday?"

"Yes sir."

"Good. Fred is in the kitchen preparing Chicken Kiev for supper. No doubt he could use an expert taster."

"Yes sir," I repeated. I made an about face and headed for the kitchen.

Fred sat at the table listening to the voices on the intercom. As I poured myself a glass of iced tea from the fridge, Hobbes was talking.

"Your credentials are credible, and I am impressed, Mr. Kirk, but I am at a loss. As a special agent for the Treasury Department, you have considerable authorityI appreciate that you have requested my help without demanding it. However, I cannot simply open my records to you." He was making a summary for my benefit, not Kirk's, and continued. "You have given me no details, nor asked specific questions. Without either, how can you expect cooperation?"

"I'm sorry, Mr. Hobbes," the voice was professional, courteous, almost pleading. "We do have reasons for secrecy, but I haven't been allowed any discretion in the matter. Not that there's much to tell, anyway."

"I, too, am sorry. It is my policy to cooperate with the authorities whenever I can reasonably do so."

There was a moment of silence, after which Kirk asked, "I need to call my office if that's okay. Does that portable phone have any extensions?"

Hobbes answered, "Make any calls you wish to. The extensions can be disabled by pressing the privacy button. Your conversation will not be overheard by anyone in this house; I shall go into the hallway while you make your call."

That was not strictly accurate. The other end of the telephone conversation was a secret to us, but Kirk's voice was clearly audible; at least it was as long as he stayed close to the desk. Hobbes didn't mention the tape recorder that was hidden in the computer room, or the mic that was concealed in the nearby bookcase. Nor did he say that he always turned it on when strangers came -- he had a remote control in his desk.

Footsteps faded away from the microphone as Kirk went to the back of the room. I could hear nothing of what was said. The boss wasn't lying.

I checked out the Chicken Kiev while we waited. Frozen entrees from the supermarket — microwave and eat.

Then I heard the sound of Hobbes wheeling himself back into his office. "Finished?" he asked.

"That was the Chicago office," Kirk's voice sounded awestruck. "My boss. He finally said, 'What the hell. We haven't gotten anywhere in forty years. Tell him.'" He shook his head. "Hard to believe. Lots of people know about it, but hardly anyone talks. Well, here it is:

"We are working on a counterfeiting case that goes back into the nineteen-fifties, when a run of almost perfect twenty dollar bills hit the street in Chicago. About a million dollars were passed in two years; then they just quit showing up."

I'm sure Hobbes and I were thinking the same thing. That was about the time the Bordens got their start.

"What about the statute of limitations?" Hobbes asked. "That was a long time ago."

"Yes, it was. The problem is that every ten years, another batch shows up. Made, we think, by the same people. They make more each time, to keep up with inflation, I suppose. A new run is on the street right now, and it may be as much as ten million."

"The same people? For forty years? Remarkable. You must have good reason for thinking so."

"We do, Mr. Hobbes. The bills are nearly perfect, but they don't age well, and after they've been used for a while they're pretty easy to spot. But the thing is this, sir; the counterfeiters are arrogant and insulting, and that is the main reason for secrecy. On about one out of every thousand bills they do this. Here, use your magnifying glass; read what it says on the seal." Kirk must have handed Hobbes a bill. We could hear the unmistakable rustle of paper money as Hobbes smoothed it out on his desk.

"Very well; 'Federal Reserve Bank of Minne...'" Hobbes paused and chuckled. "'Federal Reserve Bank of *MinnEldred* Minnesota.' Your counterfeiter has a sense of humor."

There was a long moment of silence when even our boss must have had trouble controlling his face.

"That's right," Kirk said, obviously relieved to have that revelation out of the way. "The department hopes there may be a tie-in with the Bordens and their

Eldred. Frankly, sir, I think it is a small hope, but it seems to be the only one we've got."

"And the secrecy is to avoid public embarrassment," Hobbes concluded.

"I only wanted to look at the one case, Mr. Hobbes."

"You would have found nothing, Mr. Kirk. You are too early. Very little has been recorded, other than our contract."

"Oh." His disappointment was clear. "Well, you have my card."

"Of course. I do have a question; are there other Eldred banks?"

"Not as far as I know. Probably not. In order to look right, the counterfeiter would have to stretch the six so-small letters in Eldred so that they would fill the space that MinnEldred, or Minneapolis for that matter, had taken. Right now, the twenty looks genuine. Even something as simple as a minor change in the size of the text would make it easier to spot with the naked eye."

Shortly after that, the T-man left, and I wandered back to the living room. "Do you think there's any connection?"

My boss laced his fingers across his lap. "We know little about their finances. If the Borden household and bogus money share a common ground, the treasury people should have found it, and for us to dig into it would most likely be a waste of time. Still, such a connection could help answer a question that has bothered me from the beginning, though I think it goes deeper than bogus money."

It had bothered me too, if we were thinking the same thing.

"What was their real reason for hiring me? Not to prove that Gloria is a fake. That is patently impossible. We can demonstrate that the candles were rigged, and explain the feeling of electricity, but she is unassailable. Nor can we prove the opposite because that would likewise be impossible. No, Abel, if we are to earn a fee in this case, we must learn their true motives, and profit from that knowledge."

"Any ideas?"

He took a deep breath and stretched his head back to look at the ceiling. "Yes, I have two so far: one is random and the other is useless." He didn't elaborate, but he added, "I could use a cold beer."

I nodded and a moment later put two *Fosters* on his desk.

"Are you ready for my report, Chief?" I liked the title, 'Chief.' He didn't want me to call him 'Sir,' or Mr. Hobbes, and I didn't feel comfortable calling him Car'l, especially since he had never told me what the apostrophe stood for.

He glanced at the sliding glass doors that would open onto the patio. The August sun was turning the roses on Charon's bushes to the color of new blood. He grimaced, and said, "Should I record this?"

I shook my head. The report was short. There wasn't much he didn't already know, and we finished in thirty minutes. He suggested I study the pictures — digital images, actually — from the first sitting. To save time, he said, he had cued up a series of those from the infrared camera to an interesting scene.

I went to the library where the computer was set up, and turned it on. The pictures on the monitor were pretty eerie. Designed to pick up infrared radiation, not visible light, anything that gave off heat was recorded. We never expected much from this camera, though; spectral visitors were usually described as being cold.

The images shown were in shades of fuzzy red. Candle flames were brightest, people's faces and hands were oddly distorted but recognizable, and except for reflections on the polished mahogany, the rest of the room was dark. The sequence had started just before the six candles went out, and I replayed the scene several times to get all the details. The flames of the six were blown out as if by a small blast of air, while nearly invisible wires seemed to support something around the flame of the center candle, before it too was blown out.

Then, in the darkness invisible to human eyes, Avery's left hand moved swiftly to the center of the table and found the candles. During the next few seconds, he removed something from each candle and something else from Gloria's hand, and put them all inside his jacket. "Avery, as always, will sit next to Gloria," Judith had said. So he could have a free hand, I thought.

Showmanship.

I could imagine two rubber bulbs in Gloria's hands: squeeze one and air would be forced through a tube to a manifold at the base of the candlestick, from which six more tubes would be distributed to the base of the flames — a light squeeze and they would flicker, a fast one and they would go out. The other bulb would take care of the center candle, and Avery would then clean everything up before the wood in the fireplaces was ignited. The face in the candle's flame was missing. I wondered why.

That part of the séance was the hoax, and Gloria obviously participated. But was Eldred a fake too? I shook my head. The trappings were just for atmosphere. Eldred was as real as Gloria was real, and Hobbes was right; she was unassailable.

"What do you suppose the wires were for?" I asked Hobbes later, back in his office.

"I believe they held polarized panels that acted as miniature movie screens. If you had examined the spirit room right after the séance, you'd have found two small projectors focused on the central candle, each with a film showing a face of fire. Because the face in the fire was projected on the screens, it wasn't hot enough to show up on the infrared cameras."

"Wow," I said. "How could Gloria have managed all that?"

He raised an eyebrow. "Infatuation muddles the thinking, Abel. Not Gloria. Someone outside the room."

An accomplice.

There had been only one other person in the house. No wonder she didn't think I'd find anything that first day when I searched the spirit room. She must have had some good quiet laughs, I thought wryly.

The fax machine began making noise. The fax was from Sally. She'd scrawled on the top sheet; "The best I could do. Sorry. I'm coming home." I waited while the machine spit out a dozen or so pages, and took them to Hobbes. The other sheets were a montage of short articles and pictures from old issues of the *Echo*. None of them had been in the files she had brought home from her Sunday visit with Wilder.

A few were from other periodicals.

The earlier articles were satirical, maybe even ironic: "Don't Know Where Uncle Hid the Will? Ask This Woman," said one. "Not the Ghost of a Chance!" quipped another; both poked gentle fun at the sisters. Old pictures accompanied the articles. Grainy, faded, they nonetheless showed two beautiful women, taken before Gloria started wearing a veil. But even in those you could see her look of innocence, and the beginning of Judith's icy armor.

The earliest article was dated nineteen sixty-three; the newer articles added little to what we already knew. The articles made no mention of their finances, or of Cassius, or of Regasmun. No wonder Sally had sounded depressed.

"Supper!" Fred yelled from down the hall.

"In a minute," I called back.

"This is for you, chief," I said to Hobbes, and handed him the book.

He read the title, then thumbed slowly through several pages.

"Come get it 'fore it ain't fit to eat!"

"Thank you, Abel." Hobbes said and laid the book gently on the desk.

I glanced at the title once more: *The Student's Review of Cheap North American Beers*. He liked that kind of book. Honest.

Chapter 19

Midway through supper, Sally came home. We could hear the angry roar of the engine and the squealing of tires and brakes as she parked the Lincoln in the garage. She came into the kitchen through the back door and glared at us.

"Sit yerself down and eat something," Fred told her. "I thawed out strawberries; you can have some with cream for dessert."

She ignored Fred, but told Hobbes, "I'm going to talk to Charon, see if he knows any new places." Places to her meant cemeteries. During the seven years she'd lived with Hobbes — she had moved in on what she thought was her eighteenth birthday — she had searched more than a hundred local "places," some of them repeatedly.

She faced the boss, hands on her hips, daring him. But all Hobbes said was, "He was dusting the roses for bugs. If he's not by the patio, you'll probably find him in the boathouse. You should have two hours before he leaves — he won't take the boat out until after dark."

"Eat something first," insisted the fireman.

"All right," she relented. "Maybe some strawberries."

"Not much at the *Echo?*" I asked as she was pouring cream.

"Not much. Not even with Mr. Green's help. It's as if the Bordens came out of nowhere."

"Chicago's a big town," I said. "But the past can't hide forever. Someone there knows about them. Don't give up yet."

"Easy to say." She suddenly smiled,, her mood changing completely. "But do you want to know a secret? I don't think they come from Chicago at all!"

We had all thought of that, of course. I could just as well have said, "America's a big country."

After a while, when she had finished her strawberries, Sally went to Hobbes, leaned over and gently pulled the ends of his moustache. "I'm going to talk to Charon, now. Whistle if you want something." She curtsied, winked at Fred and me, and left.

I saw her later, out by the roses. It was funny how she liked live flowers, but cut ones made her sad and depressed. But maybe not so funny, considering her passion for searching graveyards. She had no memory of her childhood or early adolescence.

What she did have was a recurring dream about a funeral home and three caskets — two opened, one closed — and a conviction that the key to her past lay hidden among the dead. Maybe it would be a name on a new headstone, or on some weathered epitaph from the past century. Or it could come from the description of a family plot on a caretaker's map. She didn't know. All she could do was to keep on searching.

After supper, Hobbes and I went into the living room. He parallel parked next to his custom-made recliner and used the overhead bars to transfer himself from his wheelchair to the only other chair in the house that he found really comfortable. He leaned back, closed his eyes, and sighed. It was a perfect position for him to sit and watch TV, but he didn't turn it on.

"I had hoped for more help from Sally." He sounded disgusted, not with Sally but with the general state of affairs. He turned to look at me; "Do we have anything for a case against *anybody?*"

"Nope," I said, "but there is always the wake. Maybe the killer will show up and his face will give him away. Or give her away," I added.

"Guilt may betray the killer in the presence of the victim? Possibly, but the four suspects we have who were around forty years ago are over sixty years old — I do not exclude Gloria — and each has developed unmatched skills of deception. Do you think one of them would let something show on his face?" He grimaced, and mocked me, "Or her face?"

"'It could happen," I insisted.

"Of course. And Lieutenant Murphy could prove that it is Marilyn who is guilty." He was joking, but it got me to thinking — Murphy just might try something like that. And we couldn't see beyond Thursday's wake, or at least I couldn't.

But Thursday was two days away; we still had to get through tomorrow, Wednesday. Clyde would be over early in the morning, and then Tom Wilder was supposed to be here at nine. At least that would pass some time.

The next morning, per Hobbes' instructions, Clyde Butler and I checked out the basement. In the southeast corner sat an ancient brick cistern that had once collected rainwater; it shared one sad-looking wall with the underside of the wide basement stairs. The brickwork under the stairs was an eyesore, and it was Hobbes' plan to cover it up with a new layer of bricks. He wanted to put in an elevator next to the stairs. After that was completed, he intended to install fitness equipment that he hoped would give him some use of his legs. A former client had gone so far as to give him a ping-pong table with a set of paddles and balls. So far, they just gathered dust. I guess we all have dreams.

Clyde studied the old brick wall. "Not much of a job here. Me and the boy can lay the new bricks Saturday, clean up and paint Monday, and still be able to leave for the Ozarks Tuesday." He thought for a minute, and then added, "But I'll need to get new bricks and mortar here before the weekend."

"Hobbes said do what you have to do."

"Good. I'll open up the old cellar door to haul the stuff in and out."

"Cellar door." What had Eldred said about a cellar? Cellar steps. Yeah. This was supposed to get my mind *off* the case.

Clyde took his measurements, made a list, and went to check the cellar door. I figured he knew what he was doing, so I went back upstairs to the kitchen for breakfast, grabbed a bowl of Fred's specialty — chilled tapioca — and a glass of juice. I took them both to the small office just off the hallway from the front door, where work could take my mind off of Fred's cooking. I turned on the notebook computer and caught up on some of Hobbes' business, but my mind kept wandering back to Gladys.

I found myself feeling grateful for Wilder and his nine a.m. appointment. He rang the doorbell right on time.

It took a few seconds to shut off my computer, slap the lid down, and slip it under my arm. I then quickly proceeded to the front door. Pulling it open a bit awkwardly, I said, "Come in."

Wilder followed me down the short hallway and into the great room. He stopped just inside the door and looked over the room as if it had been described to him in detail and he wanted to see if the description matched the real thing. Did he know that Hobbes claimed the west end near the north wall as his office and that was where he kept his desk, cabinets, and a few chairs? Did he appreciate Hobbes' keeping the whole room open; that in no way was the office area closed off from the rest of the twenty-foot by thirty-foot living space? And that if he needed real privacy, he used the small office where I had so recently been working?

Did he know that this arrangement was designed by Hobbes' just so he could navigate his wheelchair and watch the TV when he felt like it?

Wilder made no comment, but fixed his eyes on Hobbes as he slapped a copy of the offending edition of his newspaper in my hands.

Hobbes was at the other end of the great room, watching something on the screen of that oversized projection TV. When he saw us, he turned off the TV and let the curtain close over the screen. He gave us a menacing glare, which he could execute as well as anybody. Given his bald head, angular face, and droopy moustache, the menace came through well enough. The wheelchair was almost silent on the hard carpet as he rolled the length of the room to park behind the desk.

"Well, Mr. Wilder? Would you care for a coffee?"

"No thanks. This is all business. Give him the paper, Hudson." He stared at me while I studied a picture behind the boss's desk. "All right, give him the paper, *Houston!*"

I opened it to the right page and handed it to Hobbes.

"I have read it," he said. But he read it again, slowly, and out loud. "'HEZEKIAH, SHOW YOUR WORTH. PROVE YOUR GOD TO US DISBELIEVERS. Be a sacrifice.'" He looked directly at Wilder, "What kind of sacrifice is the author talking about? Your wages for a week? Your heart on a stake?" He shook his head.

"And this, 'We'll do the work, all you have to do is show up.' It reads like a newspaper advertisement, Mr. Wilder. You could have written it yourself. So I ask, did you? Is this whole thing a farce you devised to draw my attention?"

"No, Cobbs... Hobbes," Wilder almost sounded bewildered. "It's the real thing!"

"No doubt," Hobbes said, dryly. "And the rest of it, 'SEE WHAT HAPPENS: Leave an answer in the bark of the Medicine Oak at midnight. We know where you live, if you don't come to us, WE WILL COME

FOR YOU! -signed- The Witches of Meridian.' Is that the real thing, too?"

"I swear it is! I had nothing to do with writing it. That is a bona fide threat."

"All right," Hobbes said, and leaned back slightly. "I agree there is a threat, or I wouldn't have asked you here. My questions will be merely to perceive its nature.

"First, to whom or what is the threat directed? To your paper's vulnerability to law suits? Bah! To your own welfare? Nothing in the ad suggests any risk specifically to your well-being, nor does it suggest a danger to anyone else for that matter, if we exclude the reference to Hezekiah. It is vague and non-specific, even with the reference to the Medicine Oak. Such veiled threats are generally harmless. Whom would I investigate? Whom would I protect?"

Wilder seemed uncertain about giving any more details.

Hobbes waited a few seconds, then shook his head. "If you have nothing more specific, then you are wasting my time. Abel, show him the way out."

I put my hand on Wilder's shoulder, but he brushed it off.

"You're wrong, Hobbes. It is specific. It gives a name, Hezekiah. Besides, we made a deal."

"A deal where we were to see all the records about the Bordens. You gave us nothing. I can only assume you have two sets of files and you gave the meaningless one to Sally; that is why you were in no hurry to get them back." He shook his head. "And now you suggest that Hezekiah is a name of significance?"

"It is a name of significance simply because it's my middle name." He bowed slightly, "Thomas *Hezekiah* Wilder. I was named after a biblical king. Whoever put that in the paper meant it specifically for me. And whether you like it or not, we made a deal!"

"Humph," Hobbes said. He stroked the ends of his moustache, growled something that sounded like he was unhappy, and then said, "I would ask first, is your middle name common knowledge?"

"I don't broadcast it."

"Very well. Sit down and explain why you feel threatened."

If Wilder was relieved in any way, he didn't show it. He dropped into the chair I pushed over for him and started talking in a dry, raspy voice.

"A couple of months ago, the *Echo* began a series of articles about witches. At first, we simply called them harmless old women, but after a time we began offering proof that they were hoaxers and frauds and charlatans. I don't suppose you followed the series? Of course not," he said as Hobbes shook his head. "But we were doing your work. Exposing phonies. You might have appreciated that.

"But then, we added some illustrations — pictures of animal sacrifice and witches drinking blood — the usual stuff from the archives. We interviewed some practicing witches. You know there's a coven right here in Meridian? We put pictures of some of them into the *Echo,* but they were wearing their witching clothes; I don't know if any of them was recognizable."

"Get to the point," Hobbes said. "Nothing you've said so far justifies the animus of this challenge."

"The point is this: I called them useless, weak, self-deluded, and cowardly followers of Satan. I dared them to do something to prove that Satan acknowledged them; if they did, and then he did, I would put it on the front page of the *Echo*."

"So," Hobbes mused, "something happened that the witches attributed to Satan, but then you reneged on your agreement."

"Yeah," Wilder sighed. "That's it."

"What was he supposed to have done?"

"Do you follow the birth announcements in the Chicago papers?"

The boss was seldom caught off guard by anything said in that room, but that came close to doing it. He came up with a snappy reply, though. "Only at odd times, say between seldom and never. Should I read them more frequently?"

"This one made national news. Turn on your TV."

Hobbes used the remote on his wheelchair to turn the TV projector back on and to rotate it ninety degrees as the curtain over the east screen slid open — concessions to his wheelchair, so he could watch TV without leaving his desk.

"Find the news," Wilder said.

Hobbes tuned in to CNN.

"There," Wilder pointed.

A reporter was talking about the drought in Kansas.

"See it!" Wilder's voice rose. "See it! The baby! The horns, the forked tail! Tell me you see it!"

The reporter continued to talk about the drought. Whatever Wilder said he saw, I didn't see any demon baby, at least on that channel.

"Ah, yes," Hobbes said as he switched the TV off. "That is their proof? A devil's baby, Satan's child?"

"It should be enough, shouldn't it?" Wilder's voice started to fade.

"It should be, if you actually saw the child on TV, or read about it in the papers. But you have not yet acknowledged either in the *Echo*. Why not?"

"Because I don't believe it, Hobbes; I just don't believe it. The witches have done something to me... made me see things..." He glanced nervously around the room, and then lowered his voice. "Maybe not without reason. I admit we weren't too careful about the accuracy of our quotes, but they were witches, you know, and witches don't get a whole lot of respect."

Hobbes grunted his acknowledgement. He knew about the *Echo's* carelessness with the truth. It went back eighteen years to that libel suit by Hobbes against Wilder and the *National Echo*, and the resulting payment and public apology.

In a sense, Wilder had helped Hobbes. The money rescued his beginning detective agency at a time when clients were few. The notoriety brought him customers and business became brisk.

Chapter 20

But that was then. Wilder had followed Hobbes' career pretty closely after that. He had become the boss' severest critic and, paradoxically, his unintended supporter. That is not to say Wilder had mended his ways, rather, he had realized that being fair with Hobbes raised the credibility of his paper.

"Few minorities seek respect from tabloids such as the *National Echo*," Hobbes said without any particular emphasis. "But certain people might be offended by deceptions or outright lies, and threaten to retaliate. Such threats as this are not uncommon, and public printed apology often satisfies them."

He paused for effect, then added softly, "One thing must be perfectly clear; this announcement is not some fabrication of yours for publicity. Tell me it is not."

Wilder shook his head. "My god, no."

"Then, who is responsible?"

"At least thirty men and thirty-five women work in the Chicago newsroom. Any one of them could have slipped it in after the paper was supposedly ready for the printer, but before it went to press. It would have taken only seconds and a few keystrokes."

"You are saying you don't know who was responsible? Good Lord, man, you could not have been so blind."

"There are... there are some people who would have me resign from the *Echo* and move far away."

That thin smile returned briefly; he added, "That would be their second choice. The witches' approach would be their first. No, Hobbes, I'm not blind. I didn't see the person as she did it, but I know who she is. I could name her; I could even tell you what desk she works at. But I won't. I can't."

"Why not?" Hobbes' curiosity was stirred. So was mine.

"Give me a paper and pen and I'll show you."

I offered him both.

He took them and began writing. His hand moved quickly for three short words

"Her name is," and stopped.

The muscles in his hand strained as his grip tightened on the pencil; tiny drops of sweat formed on his forehead. He tried to force the pen across the paper, but it suddenly snapped between his fingers.

He dropped the pieces on the desk and leaned back. His breath was coming in short quick gasps. "Do you see? I know her name but I can't say it. I can't even write it."

"Why not, Mr. Wilder? Do you believe the witches have cast a spell on you? That you are hexed?"

"It's not funny, Hobbes. I know how strange this sounds, but I can't say her name. If we went to the office, I wouldn't be able to point out her desk. You saw my hand, saw how it fights me. Of course I'm hexed, or cursed, or something!"

"That is worthy of investigation, Mr. Wilder. So tell me, what do you want us to do?"

"I want you to send Angstrom to my Chicago office this afternoon. Have him look over all the employees and pick out the one who did this. I guarantee that he won't have any problem."

Hobbes had no difficulty translating Angstrom. He looked at me. I shrugged and said, "An hour each way, Boss."

He said, "Then, do it."

"Then..."

We were interrupted by an attack on the front door. A pounding, window-rattling demand of fist against wood that entrance be granted, which nearly drowned out the doorbell as the button was repeatedly pushed. Both were accompanied by a woman's voice screaming epithets that no lady would be likely to say.

Hobbes nodded at me. I said, "Yes sir," and made a quick trip through the short hallway to the front entrance. The noise didn't let up until I opened the door. The slender, wiry, and strong — did I say strong? The very strong middle-aged woman, who already held the screen door open with her hip, glared at me. In that split second, the largest tomcat in the world slipped between my legs and ran down the hall. The woman then simply slapped my hands, pushed me aside and strode on into the living room.

I took a second to recover from her surprise attack, and then I had to run to get between her and Hobbes.

She tried to push me a second time, but I was ready for her and gripped both of her hands. Even so, she brought them to within inches of my face. Up close, her fingernails looked like deadly weapons; I was hard put just to hold them. She might have broken free, but she suddenly relaxed and lowered her hands.

"Get out of my way. Idiot. Boob. Sycophant!" Her eyes flashed, but when I continued to block her, she turned to Wilder. "This is for you, foolish man. Catch it!" She made an underhand pitch of something invisible that Wilder seemed to catch and press against his chest. "Midnight tonight, at the Medicine Oak. You will be there or leave a message in the bark. Don't make us come after you!"

Wilder slowly collapsed onto the floor.

"Mrs. Ransom!" Hobbes said sharply.

She turned the fire in her eyes on him. "Take care that I don't send my friends after you as well. You investigate things that are none of your affair. If I were not staying with my daughter; if she hadn't pleaded with me to not cause trouble, I would show you some of those things."

"Show them!" Hobbes demanded.

"It is not you I'm after." She glared at Wilder, but when she spoke again, it was to her cat. "Come, Harmless." She shook her hands free, turned, and, with the cat following, walked down the hallway and out the door.

A few seconds passed; Fred came in from the kitchen. He had seen part of the action, but his comment was simply, "Harmless? Harmless as yer saber tooth tiger."

"Abel," Hobbes said suddenly. "Is he still alive?"

The fact was that Wilder seemed more dead than alive. He slumped down in his chair, head thrown back, eyes staring blankly at the ceiling.

I checked his pulse. It seemed strong and regular. "He's alive."

"Get him something, then. Brandy, perhaps."

A few minutes later, Wilder seemed almost back to normal. "What did she throw at me?"

"Nothing as far as we could see," Hobbes said, and then added, "Could she be the one responsible for this?" He held up the paper.

"No, but keep her away from me anyway."

"Very well. Now, if you will write a letter authorizing Abel to visit your offices in Chicago, he will be on his way."

"Yeah," I added, "and be sure you spell Angstrom right. It's H-o-u-s-t-o-n."

Fifteen minutes later, I had checked my Beretta to be sure it was loaded and slipped it into my shoulder holster. I usually carried it with me on strange assignments; this one definitely qualified. I backed the Town Car out of the garage and drove as far as the corner McDonalds, where I picked up a Happy Meal — my definition of a Happy Meal was any meal Fireman Fred hadn't prepared — and then aimed the car toward the great metropolis. It was early afternoon and traffic was light; by one-thirty, I was walking into the outer office of the *Echo*. I approached the receptionist.

Her nametag said she was Pamela Ravenkill.

I introduced myself; she seemed happy to see me and said I should call her Pam. Her voice was deep and raspy, almost like that of a man who smoked too much, but her smile was full of perfect teeth — bright, dazzling and unnaturally white. It disappeared when I showed her Wilder's letter.

"I've been expecting you. Mr. Wilder called and said you were coming, and that I should give you whatever help you want." She lowered her eyes as if she was embarrassed. "He said you were looking for a witch."

"I thought so up till now," I tried to look apologetic, but I supposed I was too surprised. "Do you know of any?"

"I wouldn't dare to name her if I did, Mr. Houston, but Mr. Wilder said you would know her yourself, once you saw her." Her smile suddenly brightened the room. "You have an opportunity to see how a great newspaper works. Go through that door and you'll find its very heartbeat."

I went where she pointed, not knowing what to expect. A door opened to a remarkably small elevator. Two people would have been uncomfortable using it together. Even before I stepped inside, tendrils of claustrophobia started tickling my backbone. I inhaled a lung-full of air, held it for ten seconds, and regained control. I stepped inside and looked around quickly, but not even the fire extinguisher and gas mask enclosed in glass surprised me.

It was just an elevator.

"Press 'B'," she called after me. Elevators did not usually bother me, but in this one, the claustrophobia became acute as soon as the door had closed and the elevator began moving down. I held my breath, while blood pounded in my ears; I counted out sixty seconds. The pounding almost drowned out the recorded voice that came from somewhere in the background. Bits came through. "Hobbes, Hobbes," something "Hobbes." Whispering... Whispering... Then it stopped. A faint alarm went off somewhere. I shook my head and the alarm faded.

My head cleared and I felt only a mild fogginess — probably nothing new to me.

The elevator finally stopped and the door opened. I stepped into the newspaper's land of make-believe — a place where Elvis sightings were commonplace and Martians abducted backwoods and shoeless maidens, where dogs were telepathic, and clairvoyants commonly told the future with uncanny accuracy. This was the dream world where half a dozen men and women worked at desks full of dirty ashtrays and coffee stains, as they researched the legends and myths of urban society, and where they made them believable and ready for tomorrow's newspaper.

I cautiously started to breathe again and let Pam, who must have come down the stairs, take my hand and lead me through a corridor past the make-believers and into the real newspaper's busy office. I didn't count them, but at least fifty desks had computer terminals with people working at them. Two or three girls glanced up and nodded; otherwise, everyone ignored me.

"Look over there," Pam pointed at a corner desk. "Doesn't she look like your neighbor, Linda

Butler? She's the witch. See her pointed hat and the broom leaning against the wall?" The girl hardly glanced at me.

I didn't see a pointed hat or a broom. What I did see was a desk half covered with stuffed cats and dogs. The old familiar itching on my hands came back, but faded when I realized that was all there was. There weren't any weasels or rats to go with them.

Pam then asked an odd question; "Do you know the Vulcan salute?"

I nodded.

"Do it." She said it as a command.

I held up my hand, middle finger separated from the ring finger.

"Okay," she said. "Forget I told you to do that."

I stared at her for a second, "Forget what?"

"Nothing important."

I must have had a puzzled look on my face, but she simply smiled and said, "Well, you've seen enough now. It's time to go."

She didn't rush me though. She let me wander around for fifteen minutes before she led me back to the elevator and sent me up by myself. Again, I held my breath for sixty seconds. The door opened, and I returned to the lobby. A different receptionist waved at me as I left the building.

So did the two women who were slipping into costumes.

"Office party tonight," one of them said.

I glanced back through the glass door.

One girl was dressing as a gray long-tailed rat. The other was changing into a sleek brown weasel outfit.

I shook my head — my thinking was a little foggy. What had I really seen? Stuffed cats and dogs and a couple dressing up as a rat and a weasel for a party.

Big deal. The animals didn't mean a thing.

But the more I thought about the way Pam had acted, the more obvious it became that she believed that I had been hypnotized. But why? To get me to believe that Linda Butler was the true witch we had been looking for? What the heck was going on?

I had forgotten that the Chicago expressways had only two season — winter, and construction. This one was construction. It was past eight o'clock by the time I parked the car in Hobbes' driveway.

A couple of stray dogs ran silently across the back yard. They were big dogs. Again I thought, "Big deal."

When I entered Hobbes's office, he was watching the traffic conditions, but he turned the TV off and listened closely to my report. He stroked the ends of his moustache four times each before I was halfway through. I almost never saw him that agitated. There wasn't anything in my report to cause that kind of a reaction as far as I could tell, so I went on.

"You know what I think, Chief? I think Wilder had somebody try to hypnotize me so that I would think Linda Butler was a witch. It didn't work. If anyone was a witch, it was Pamela Ravenkill."

"I see. They tried to use gas on you, but you anticipated that and held your breath? That was very perceptive of you, Abel." He nodded his approval. "When you were delayed on your journey home, I attempted to make contact with Wilder at the *Echo,* although he had left here shortly after you did. I was told that he and Miss Ravenkill had left the office about five o'clock, but that neither of them had called in nor answered their pages since then.

"Nevertheless, I would like for you to slip onto the MerSH grounds and be near the Medicine Oak at midnight. Arm yourself. I do not yet know what is going on. Wilder might show up at midnight or the writer of that newspaper challenge might appear. In any case you should be prepared."

Hobbes started to say something more, but then he suddenly stopped, closed his eyes, gripped the wheels of his chair and started rocking back and forth. I recognized it as a variation on a theme of Nero Wolf's, the great fictional detective. It meant he was seeing something no other mortal could see. It also meant don't interrupt. Two minutes passed before he opened his eyes. "We have clients coming tomorrow?"

"No," I said. "But, we have the wake to go to."

He nodded and closed his eyes again.

The doorbell rang; at the same time, Fred called out that he had a late supper ready for me.

Chapter 21

I had hoped it was the pizza man, but it was only Clyde and Richie Butler from next door.

Clyde smiled wryly, "I hear my mother-in-law stopped by this morning. We'd like to apologize to you and Mr. Hobbes."

I shook my head, "None needed. She has a certain amount of charm."

His smile became broad, covering his whole face. "I bet. We still need to talk to Mr. Hobbes about the elevator. If he's free."

I motioned for them to follow me and turned toward the kitchen. A look of alarm crossed Clyde's face. "I don't want to interfere with your supper." He had eaten Fireman Fred's cooking once.

"It would be our pleasure to share it with you. There may not be much, and it's not much better than nothing." I lowered my voice. "But we can call out for pizza later."

"Oh, yeah," he said quickly. "I just remembered. Katya is frying chicken. It's not bad."

"Fireman Fred and his microwaved meatloaf or Katya Ransom and her fried chicken," I said thoughtfully. "I think I'd take the meatloaf."

"Not if you would have to explain why to Katya Ransom, you wouldn't."

Richie added, "And then listen to her tell you about the evil of wasting food. But, you know something? Her cooking ain't that bad, if she just doesn't talk too much while we're trying to eat."

We found Hobbes in the kitchen sitting in his wheelchair, staring glumly at the plate in front of him. I was wrong about the meatloaf. Fred had made ham salad sandwiches instead, and had put out potato chips, pickles and dip. I could almost see visions of pizza flashing through the boss' head.

"While we're here," Clyde cut into Hobbes' reverie. "I thought we'd take a look at your basement to see about putting in that elevator you've been talking about. We should have done it last spring, but, well, you know."

Clyde's wife, Jane, had died in a fall at Starved Rock State Park in January. Clyde and Jane had agreed many years ago that if one died while they were still young, the other would be free to marry — if the right person came along.

The right person turned out to be Linda Ransom, whom he had known in high school; they had become reacquainted at Jane's funeral. Five months later, they had married.

When I spoke to Richie about his new stepmother, all he would say was, "I'm glad Dad is happy." Then he would add a disclaimer about Katya and Linda's brother, Luke; "Dad would be better off if they weren't around so much."

Personally, all I could say was that Linda was close to being the most beautiful woman I'd ever seen, and she was charming, intelligent and witty. I would have married her myself except for three reasons; but darned if I can remember what they were.

Chapter 12

Clyde and Richie had just come up from the basement when Hobbes mentioned that maybe I shouldn't go to the Medicine Tree alone tonight. Richie immediately volunteered to go with me. Hobbes and Clyde exchanged glances, and Clyde said, "Okay."

Hobbes made his thumb, finger and fist into a symbolic gun, positioned so that only I could see it, and then shook his head.

Earlier in the day, Hobbes had said I should take a gun. Now I shouldn't? Something had changed; apparently, Hobbes' no longer considered my planned adventure to be dangerous. He wouldn't have set it up so that the boy could come with me, otherwise.

I didn't ask him why, and he didn't volunteer to tell me, but I handed him my pistol and holster. He slipped them into his desk drawer.

The Medicine Tree was an ancient tree made up mostly of folklore and legend, but with just enough fact thrown in to make some of the legend believable. The fact was that, during the early 1900's, the hospital's administration had allowed one doctor to practice a simple and pragmatic therapy; if a patient had refused to take his medicine, he had been shackled to the tree and left there with neither food nor drink until he had changed his mind. Rumor had it that a hundred patients had endured that treatment — some for hours, none for more than a day and a night. Then, one man had been tied to the tree on Good Friday and left there, forgotten, until Easter Sunday. Wild dogs had found him and had tried to keep him warm and alive by covering him with their bodies. They had remained there until two patients walking by that Sunday morning had seen them and called security. The guards drove the animals away, but the man's body had already turned cold.

It had been the dogs, not the dead man that had first made the news. But, it had been the use of the Medicine Tree that had caused one doctor to be dismissed, and the administrator to be replaced.

The legend had started then and had grown. It said that bark low to the ground had turned dark brown as the blood turned old; the blood that had come from patients who had rubbed their skin raw trying to escape. They had feared the great wild dogs that roamed the nearby forests, now known as Starved Rock State Park. Some patients had disappeared completely, leaving only the chain that had once held them — the chain and the unopened shackle. Stories had been added, and, as the years passed, had been forgotten.

Rumor said that witches had come to hold their Sabbaths around that tree. They had sometimes left messages to the coven wedged in its bark.

Most of the legend had faded away. Only the witches remained.

And now, a century old, the tree stood by itself near the eastern edge of the hospital grounds not far from the river. The tree was a wiry, ugly and deformed oak of uncertain species. No other living thing near its size and stature grew within a hundred feet. It was surrounded instead by a dense jumble of bushes and saplings that grew eagerly in the spring, turned brown in the summer, and died in the fall. The only area where the undergrowth had been beaten down and cleared away was immediately around the trunk.

I had misgivings about a fifteen-year old boy keeping me company in a place where a man's life was supposedly already forfeit. Hobbes though, was encouraging it, so he must have a better idea of what was happening than I did. As far as my pistol was concerned, he didn't think handguns and teen-age boys went together. Rifles and shotguns were okay, but not pistols.

As a result, somewhere around eleven p.m., Richie and I, sans firearm, found ourselves settling in among some dense brush and tall weeds about fifty feet from the tree. We used our flashlights only to avoid poison ivy. Clouds drifted across the moon, making it vanish and reappear; the light it provided was weak and sickly. Fred had made some sandwiches of bologna, cheese, and mustard on dry white bread; he had thoughtfully wrapped them in cloth to avoid the rattle of paper bags. We washed the sandwiches down with two thermos bottles of hot coffee, as we sat back and waited.

We talked for a while about the Cubs and the Sox, keeping our voices low and one ear attuned to the sounds around us; the rustle of wind in the leaves, the chirp of a cricket, and the far-off baying of a hound. The closer to midnight, the quieter we became until we were barely whispering.

And then the boy suddenly asked me, "What do you think about Linda?"

"Your step-mother? She seems all right, I guess. Why?"

"It just seems like they got married so soon after Mom died."

"Oh," I said, and thought for a minute. I wanted to give him a reasonable answer but step-son, step-mom problems were a bit out of my area. Maybe he felt lonely since he had lost his mom and now had to share his dad. Maybe it was something else. The best I could do was ask questions and let him talk his way through. "How long did they know each other?"

"Since high school, and then Mom met her again a couple of months before she... before she died. And after she died, Linda moved right in on Dad. They just got married too soon, Abel. Didn't they?"

"I don't know, but does having Katya as a step-grandmother help?"

He didn't answer right away. When he did, it was with a short laugh. "Could be. Yeah, considerate, sensitive Grandma. She helps a lot."

"Shhh," I held a finger up. "Someone is coming."

Feet, heavy on the weeds and brush, tramped their way to the beaten-down circle around the Medicine Tree. It was impossible to count them, but the feet might have belonged to a dozen people. Two of those people carried kerosene lanterns that they hung from low branches. All wore white cloaks and white pointed hats with wide brims that drooped over their faces — all but one, who was cloaked in black, and whose hat was black and loose and floppy.

A coven of witches had appeared.

One stretched her arms around the Medicine Tree; a second took her hands from the opposite side. Together, they began a dance counter-clockwise around the tree, singing, "Round about the cauldron go; in the poisoned entrails throw." They ended with laughter, their joy of the night reaching out across Richie and me and fading into the river.

"Enough!" said the one in black. "We have business to attend to." Her voice was cold, sharp, and commanding.

The command was endorsed by one in white, "Hear, hear!" And the coven became quiet.

The one in black said, "He is not here and no message is fastened to the bark. What do we do?"

"Must we do anything?" One of the other's asked. "His paper printed a retraction and an apology. That's more than most would do."

"That's right," said another. "We have been persecuted beyond endurance already. But if a man dies, it can only become worse."

"And our dancing at the Tree would come to an end," said the first.

"Who put that terrible thing in the paper, anyway?" the second asked bitterly. "I've talked to each of the coven; none of us did. We wouldn't know how to do it, anyway. It had to be Wilder, and that's why he's not here."

The one in black spoke with sudden relish, "No. Not Wilder. He wrote the amusing, entertaining, harmless stories about our kind that people liked to read, but that few believed. That's true enough. But he didn't write that terrible challenge for sacrifice. It wasn't him. He wouldn't do something that would hurt *his* newspaper, and that writing has indeed caused it great harm.

"Oh, no, it could only have been one person — our greatest enemy and you all know who he is. I've already sent him the warnings."

There was a puzzled silence in the coven. "Warnings?" someone said finally.

"Yes, warnings. Harmless things in themselves. Symbols of our sisters, one at midnight for four midnights!"

"But the sisters..."

"Wilder has called us frauds and fakes," the leader in black said, raising her voice. "But he is not the one who told the big lie and delivered that challenge. No, it was not him. I speak of the one who calls himself a detective and would use the law against us!"

"A detective?" the first white said slowly. "Car'l Hobbes?"

"Car'l Hobbes!" some of them repeated with sudden anger.

"And he's not alone," the leader said clapping her hands together. "The one we hate above all others. The one who killed three of our sisters. He is with him!"

"Abel Houston!" they cried out, and then became silent as the leader raised her hand. "But tonight... tonight we have our revenge. Tonight, Hobbes and Houston pay!"

Richie sucked in his breath, "What...?" he said, almost in a stage whisper.

"Someone's there!" the leader cried, spinning around. "Who's there? Who's there?" She grabbed a lantern from the tree and began searching for us. Richie and I were frozen in place. What could the two of us do against a dozen of them? She raised the lantern high as she tried to see beyond the light. As it swung back and forth above her head, the floppy hat flopped and I saw a face twisted in hatred — a face exulting in vengeance for wrongs from the distant past. In seconds, she would see mine.

"Houston," she whispered. "Houston, Abel Houston. You're here, aren't you?" She came closer.

For an instant, I wondered why Hobbes had changed his mind about my bringing a gun. But now it was too late to worry about that. I tensed my muscles, ready to jump and run.

Chapter 22

And then a familiar voice spoke loudly and with her usual sarcasm. "Don't be such an idiot, you whiny, puny excuse for a witch! Use your second sight, not that pathetic lantern! Close your eyes and look. I just did, and no one's there!" Katya Ransom, the only witch we really knew, had come unknowingly to our rescue.

The leader turned around sharply, her body trembling in sudden fury. She strode halfway around the tree to face her accuser. "You... you..."

"Don't stammer like an imbecile, you cretinous excuse for a mistress of witches! Speak out. Tell us all how much of a leader you are!"

"Go! Go! Go!" She began pushing Katya into the brush, away from us. The rest of the witches stared in disbelief, and then followed the pair.

"Go, go, go," I whispered to Richie. We ran from the Medicine Tree.

At least, now we knew two of the witches.

And then, I wondered why Wilder hadn't come. I wondered why I even thought of him. Finally, I wondered what she meant by, "Tonight, Hobbes and Houston pay."

We ran until we were safely away. When we had walked enough to get our breath, Richie asked me the obvious questions, "Why do they hate you? Why are they afraid of you?"

"It's all a misunderstanding, Richie. I'll tell you about it sometime."

For a moment, it looked like Richie might press for more, but then he shrugged and we walked the rest of the way home in silence. I saw him to his door and then went home myself.

It was well past midnight; the lights were still on in the great room. I took the elevator up, thinking that Hobbes was waiting up for me and watching something on the big screen. When I stepped into the room, though, it wasn't Hobbes that I saw sitting in his wheelchair in his usual place. Thomas Hezekiah Wilder had taken over the wheelchair and was sitting there mumbling. The patio doors slipped open; three cats danced in on silent feet. They were followed by three rats, who studied me with black beady eyes. Weasels entered and began prowling around, sniffing the air. They turned and hissed at the dogs that had somehow placed themselves between the cats and me. The dogs bared their long canine teeth.

The coven had come. They were here for revenge. They danced around me in wild silence, mouths drooling, ready to attack, waiting for the command.

Miniature horns suddenly appeared on Wilder's forehead. They began to grow. The demon was taking over. I had only seconds.

Blood began pounding in my ears, but the voice that I couldn't hear in the elevator became perfectly clear.

"Hobbes, he killed Hobbes, killed Hobbes, kill Hobbes." The voice repeated itself and repeated and repeated. I rushed to Hobbes' desk and took my pistol from the drawer. I turned and strode back to Wilder. The animals followed me, step by step. They crowded around in a circle that grew tighter with each second. Claustrophobia began to take over with its cold sweat and rising panic. Wilder opened his mouth, started to talk, to put a curse on me. I pointed my pistol and shot him, and shot him again, and again — seven times I shot him — point blank to the head. It was amazing how quiet the Beretta was; there was so little blood. Actually, no blood at all.

The animals faded away. Strong hands took the pistol from me. Strong hands laid me on a couch and let me sleep.

A face from the past haunted my dream. A twisted face full of hatred. A weasel. A survivor from the coven that I had helped destroy twenty years ago. She would always be around.

A young face. One that was now Pamela Ravenkill.

A comforting voice told me to forget her; she was only bitter and could not harm me.

My sleep became deep and restful.

I slept until noon, got up, showered, shaved and put on a dark suit that was appropriate for a wake. I would have worn my NASA tie, but it was being held as evidence. In its place, I put on a silk tie showing a rocket ship blasting off into space. I'd found it at a garage sale when I had still been in high school, but had never worn it. It somehow seemed fitting.

Vague memories of a really bad dream kept coming back to me. At one point in the dream, I had been drugged into thinking I wasn't drugged. At another, Hobbes had emptied the bullets from my pistol so no one could get hurt. He had said, in my dream, that I had spent too much time coming home from Chicago. He had said that I had to be allowed to carry out the post-hypnotic commands to be rid of them. The dream had ended with someone saying that everything was all right, and that I could forget the dream.

Early Thursday evening, when I let Hobbes off at the main entrance to the *Harmes-Nobel Chapel* on North Division and parked the Lincoln in a nearly full parking lot, I felt optimistic. A lot of cars — a lot of people — a lot of leads. I was sure somebody there could tell us something about Gladys' past. I found a seat next to my boss and waited for things to get started.

Bits of that bad dream kept trying to get my attention, but then Hobbes would say something, and for a while, the dream would become forgettable again.

Sally would have been impresses. Flowers were everywhere — a hundred vases of them surrounded the casket and lined the walls. More than a hundred, the majority of them far from modest. I would never have guessed that Gladys had so many friends.

Hobbes had already approached the casket and was studying the thin face that slept before him. I made my way to his side and whispered my apology to her. His words were a little stronger. "Miss Gladys Kelly Jones," he said softly. "Whether or not I could have done something to save your life, I don't know. However, I shall mourn your passing, and I pledge vengeance for you. Insofar as it is possible for me to do so, I shall unmask your killer and bring that person to justice."

"Amen," I added.

The wake was scheduled to begin at six — about the time we got there, but a long line of people was already waiting to speak to the family. Hobbes and I positioned ourselves so we could watch those who talked to the Bordens, and see their faces as they paid their respects to the departed. A pattern, with few exceptions, quickly became clear. A middle aged man or woman would nod to Avery, ignore Cassius, speak briefly to Judith, and give Gloria a tearful hug. Gloria would say a few words — a gossamer thin black veil barely shielding her eyes. The mourner would take both of her hands and murmur words of condolence, then turn and walk away. Very few people looked at the coffin or at the modest remains that rested inside.

I looked at Hobbes. "Hardly seems fair."

He grimaced. "People from past séances, no doubt —— hopeless dreamers who look to Gloria for reassurance about their own dead." He sucked in a deep breath and gritted his teeth. "Half of them wouldn't have recognized Gladys if they passed her on the street."

"Worshippers for Saint Gloria," I muttered.

We stayed till half past nine, which was when the last visitor left. Of the two hundred or so who passed by, only five spent any time at the casket. Gladys had been one in a group of volunteers who visited patients at a nursing home; the coming of those five — also volunteers — provided the only clue that she had ever had any life away from the house on Belleview.

Cassius was the first of the family to say farewell to his friend of forty-five years. He gazed at her for few moments, placed his fingers against his lips and then touched her forehead, transferring a gentle kiss. He was followed by Avery, who paused and sighed before moving on. The older man looked pale and drawn, the two faint scars visible against a bloodless cheek. Judith was the most surprising. She wept openly as she faced the casket. A chink in her cold-blooded armor? Did she really care for the little housekeeper?

Gloria raised her veil, smiled at the body, and tilted her head — sharing a secret, I thought. My hands began to itch.

I followed Hobbes outside. He waited while I brought the car around and pulled up beside him. I let him get in by himself, then I stowed the wheelchair in the back seat, got in, revved the engine, and jerked away from the curb.

"Well, Abel," he said, finally, "Did you see the face of the killer?"

"Yes," I replied. "The face was there. I just don't know which one it was. Did you have any better luck?"

"I found only disappointment. I had hoped to confirm some older conjectures but there was nothing. Certainly nothing I could take to court."

Now, what the heck did he mean by that? Did he already think he knew who the murderer was? I shook my head slightly. With him, you never knew.

We were home by eleven-thirty p.m., and were greeted at the door by Sally, who was literally bouncing with excitement. For half an hour, we listened as she talked about an ancient cemetery she had visited earlier that day. It was almost buried in an overgrown wooded area, where a church had once flourished. The oldest gravestone she could read had said Charles Applewhite, Beloved Husband — 1826-1896. The cemetery harbored *three* families, she said, *thirty-one* stones, all covered by weeds and surrounded by giant oak trees. She had taken careful notes on names and dates and had already entered the information into her computer database.

Her enthusiasm lessened, though, when she talked about tomorrow's work. "It's update time," she said, "for the *Walnut Grove* cemetery, and I have to be there to record the additions. That will probably take all morning."

Hobbes said, "Take whatever time you need. Our investigation has stalled. I cannot think of anything you can do here."

The next day, the hours from morning into afternoon were marked by grumpy comments and snide remarks from him to me, and me to him. Sometimes, griping like that developed into an idea that led somewhere. Not this time.

Several times during the day, Hobbes called the *Echo*. Neither Tom Wilder nor Pamela Ravenkill had reported in, and, no, they didn't know when either one would be there.

That afternoon, a small load of red brick and buckets of mortar were delivered and stored in the basement. At about five p.m., Clyde and Richie finished their painting; they left with promises to start on the cistern come Monday, after the paint had had plenty of time to dry.

Hobbes watched them walk across the back yard. "I don't see Sally's Bronco, Abel. It's unlike her to be this late." He didn't ask if she'd left a message with anyone. In this household, messages were always relayed.

"Yeah," I agreed. "She got you worried, Chief?"

He nodded. "Moderately. We still have some daylight left. Take a quick look at the *Walnut Grove* cemetery and see if Sally is there; speak to the caretaker if needed."

The cemetery was three or four miles west of town and another three miles, mostly south but partly west, on a winding Route 15. I might have enjoyed getting out and going there, but Sally came home before I had even reached the Lincoln. She didn't look any happier than anyone else, as I accompanied her into the house.

We stopped by the kitchen in time to hear Fred telling Hobbes that he'd found some bologna and cheese subs at the deli and already had a German chocolate cake thawing out, and supper would be in an hour.

"No, Fred," Hobbes said. "There will be no bologna and cheese sandwiches tonight. If you will set up the grill by the boat landing, I will barbecue steaks that Abel will go out and purchase for me. And the whole household, including you and Sally and Charon, will eat steak and drink beer and forget about the damn case." To me he added, "And get coleslaw, fruit salad, Italian bread from Kroger's' deli, and baked potatoes from Wendy's if they still have them."

I made a mental note to also get some beer that cost more than eight dollars a case as I headed for the car.

So it was, as darkness fell, that we sat at the picnic table like normal people, as we ate, and drank, and laughed.

Chapter 23

It was inevitable that talk would turn to the case, at some point. Charon, who was feeling mellow, asked us to tell him a little about it. Hobbes said maybe we should. Some of the cobwebs might get blown away if we talked over everything as a group. After about two hours of listening, when the full moon was bright, and he was about to doze off, Charon suddenly jerked up, the end of his white beard jutting forward and down like the nose of a hound hot on a scent. "Tell me what Eldred said again," he demanded, "About the water and the clock."

We told him: "Clock, water, a full moon, a house with cellar steps. Twins." Charon listened. Then, he stood up and took a few steps down the bank until he was between us and the river.

"I don't know nothin' about twins, but ye're all missing the boat about the rest of the stuff, and you know what? It's going to take the boatman to get you on board." He chuckled. "Don't any of you see it? It's why they all came way out here. The water and the clock ain't in Chicago." He made a grand sweep with his arm, at the river, and across it. "There's your water they're all talking about. I see it every night and know every inch from the sand bars to the dam. And there, on the other side, is your clock!"

The four of us stared across the river at Meridian's best–known landmark –– the sixty–foot tall, century–old clock tower. Its four faces stared mutely off in all directions, a part of the history of the institution that had helped define the city. The tower had been built in the 1860's as a symbol of the Midwest's humane treatment for dealing with the insane. But the symbol had been meaningless; the hospital had been anything but humane. Local historians said it had suffered from the "Mad Doctor Syndrome," where all–powerful doctors did countless medical experiments on helpless patients.

Ten years after it had opened, scandals had caused the state legislature to all but abandon the Meridian facility; the population that had been expected to reach six thousand had never exceeded four hundred. Embarrassed politicians had been unable to close the hospital, but they eventually built a new one in Kankakee as the Meridian hospital faded into obscurity. But the clock was still there. It stood tall and visible up and down the Illinois River. I had seen it hundreds of times from my bedroom window and heard it strike countless hours.

"And there's your moon!" Reflected across the slow-moving summer river –– a romantic moon, a lovers' moon –– and now, a killer's moon.

Hobbes and I, as one, looked from the river to the house, toward the cellar steps. It was easy to picture Gloria and Judith standing there. A minute later, I could see one of them, I couldn't tell which, holding an ax.

We let the puzzle of why they came to Meridian and Car'l Hobbes piece itself together. The pieces fit. Until now, it hadn't made much sense –– regardless of what Judith had said. Come to think of it, did it make any more sense now? Why even bring up the forty–year old, all but forgotten disappearance of a man whom no one claimed to know? That was the real question, and it had little to do with proving that Gloria was or wasn't a genuine spiritualist.

Probably five minutes passed before Hobbes spoke.

"We have no proof that you're right, Charon, but I have no doubt that you are." Hobbes looked up at the moon and tugged gently at the ends of his moustache. "Yes, four decades ago, Judith and Gloria Borden stood by some cellar steps and looked at that same moon; pictures had been taken by a friend, probably Gladys. Some of them showed the river and the clock tower, but others undoubtedly showed something much more suggestive. We may never know what. But what they showed was revealing enough to kill for. They probably did not show Eldred's murder, or where he was buried. Nothing so obvious. At the moment, it's pointless to speculate, but just knowing there were pictures may be all we need."

"Sure, Chief. He was buried under a concrete floor in somebody's basement without them knowing about it, and forty years later, he brought the Borden ladies back with their attorney to find out who killed him! And why would he do that?" I shook my head. "Answer unknown."

Hobbes nodded. "We have a difficult situation, compounded by the fact that part of the premise is impossible. Eldred is dead. He cannot talk in any fashion, so obviously someone else is directing their actions. Who?"

"It has to be Judith, Avery, or Gloria."

"Perhaps, but you should not discount Cassius, or even Marilyn."

I didn't answer. Though I hated to admit it, some of the most successful killers were the ones who looked the most unlikely.

Hobbes continued, "Is it possible that he is buried under this house?"

I shook my head. Yesterday's check of the basement with Clyde was still clear in my mind. "That floor is the original cement, and it's as old as the house. Nobody has been buried in that basement in the last hundred years. I guarantee it."

Hobbes settled back, silent for a moment, thinking. "The mystery of Eldred and the Bordens has its beginning somewhere on River Street; the solution to Gladys' murder will be found here also. It could be in any house along the river that has a view of the clock. Local history, the library, the courthouse will tell us a lot. That is, if we have indeed boarded the right boat." He inclined his head toward Charon, who nodded back.

"Mr. Hobbes," Sally said. "What was the name of the funeral home?"

"The Harmes-Noble Chapel, Sally. Is that important?"

"Perhaps. I may have seen your first physical tie-in to Meridian."

Hobbes looked at her with eyes narrowed; the air suddenly felt charged in anticipation. "Yes?"

"There was a hearse at the Walnut Grove cemetery this morning. It came without any procession, just by itself. A burial crew unloaded a casket and put it in the ground. A priest said something over the grave, then he left, and they shoveled the dirt in. The thing was, the hearse had a Chicago address, and it was strange to me that it would come all the way down here alone. Somehow, I got the sense that someone was trying to fulfill an obligation but keep the trip secret at the same time."

"And the name on the hearse, Sally?"

"It was," she said slowly and for effect, "*Harmes-Noble Chapel.*"

Chapter 24

Sometimes, being a detective can be downright exhilarating; but never more than when you get that first break, and we'd just been given not one, but two. I could sense the sudden euphoria gripping the five of us; moonlight was reflecting in the eyes of my friends.

Hobbes, though, had questions. "Was there a marker?"

"No, and there won't be for a few days. But I think the grave may have been in a family plot."

"Was the family name 'Jones?'"

She shook her head. "But I know the caretaker."

"I suppose it's too late to see him tonight?"

"It's midnight," she answered.

"Early in the morning, then, Sally. Visit your friend at the cemetery and pry from him whatever you can." To the rest of us he said, "Tomorrow, we shall no doubt find many things to do. Tonight, we can have a small celebration. More beer, Fred! Abel, is there any fruit salad left?"

I dreamed of sirens that night, and woke up Saturday with a cheap North American beer headache, even though I hadn't drunk any of the cheap stuff. I stumbled down to the kitchen. Hobbes was enjoying Pop-Tarts and coffee for breakfast; he seemed pleased to see me, but he smiled grimly.

"Why do you suppose none of our clients alluded to the simple fact that they were connected to Meridian?" he asked.

"They haven't lived around here for forty years. Maybe they felt it didn't matter."

"No, Abel, I disagree. They required proof of fraud, or of substance to Gloria's claim. I could have provided neither without digging deeply into the past. Regasmun and Judith Borden would have known that."

"Yeah," I muttered.

"I submit a challenge to you, Abel. I will call and demand the presence of all the Bordens and Regasmun here this afternoon. The demand will be reinforced by the threat of revealing our small knowledge to Lieutenant Murphy. I will meet with the two elder Bordens and their lawyer, while you walk with Marilyn by the river."

"And the challenge?"

"To see which of us will learn more. You by charm and wit, or me by guile and threat."

"You're on, Boss."

"One more thing. I wish to honor my agreement with Forrest Green; I'd like for you to keep him informed, even though the archives of the *National Echo* may not extend to this county and he will most likely be of limited help. As to the future, who knows? He may become our most valuable asset in the media."

"Yes sir." I wondered if Green played poker.

Hobbes poured his second or third coffee into a travel mug and placed it, along with an apple, on the tray in front of him, spun his wheelchair around, and left for the office. Fred wasn't there to give me an angry look, so I fixed myself an omelet, poured some coffee, and wondered what I'd say to Marilyn.

Breakfast finished, I called Forrest. He seemed pleased to hear from me, so we chatted for a moment. He concluded with, "Thank you, me boy. I'll drop around the *Echo* this morning. If I find anything helpful, I'll be glad to call you."

After I hung up the phone, I ambled into the office to see if Hobbes had any success with his calls. He looked up and said, "Judith, Gloria, and Avery will be here about two o'clock, Cassius at three, and Marilyn at four. Their choices, not mine."

At that moment, Sally came in. She stopped in front of the desk and shook her head. "Nothing," she said flatly.

Hobbes leaned forward, surprised, but not speechless. "Nothing? Impossible. There is never nothing."

"You weren't there," she said defensively. "You didn't talk to Digger." *Digger* was the name she gave to any cemetery caretaker. "The burial was prearranged in nineteen seventy eight, before he was hired. All he had was a name on the plot map, 'Gladys K. Jones,' and instructions from the funeral home. There was not another Jones within a hundred yards of her grave. I checked."

He drummed his fingers against the desk. "What about the *Harmes-Noble* chapel?"

"When I called from Digger's, a man said they followed a contract paid for nineteen years ago. They had nothing more."

"No, Sally. There is much more. Certainly, there is enough to bring five people down from Chicago, and by this evening we will know what some of that is."

He turned to me. "Ask Fred to come in here, Abel. The day is young, and I believe we can start Sally and him on our local search for the history of the Bordens."

Later, after they had their instructions and had embarked on the quest, I left Hobbes in the library looking for a place for his new book. I wandered outside in search of Charon. I found him in the boathouse studying the insides of a trolling motor someone had given him four or five years ago. It had never worked, and he had taken it apart to see if he could fix it. The mechanics of it defied him, so he'd never put it back together, but he stared at it now and then.

He raised his shaggy eyebrows and pointed his long nose at me, like a cannon. "It'll never replace oars."

"Never," I agreed. "Think you'll ever fix it?"

"Never." He grinned at me. "That would defeat my purpose in keeping it."

"Symbol of the modern world?"

"Exactly."

"Charon, old friend," I said after a moment's reflection, "You've been around a long time; maybe you can answer a question."

"Been around longer than the hills. Older than dirt. What do you want to know?"

I told him about Marilyn; and my wondering why she hadn't told me about her part in the séances.

"Ain't been around long enough to understand women, young fellow. Nobody has. But, maybe she was being loyal to her family. Maybe it just weren't too important."

Loyalty I understood.

A chauffeured limousine stopped in front of the old house just before two p.m.; a uniformed driver got out and opened the back door. Avery stepped out first, then he assisted Judith and Gloria. He held Gloria's arm as they came up the walk. Out of the corner of my eye, I noticed that the curtains over one of our next door neighbor's windows moved slightly; I thought I caught a glimpse of Katya Ransom, but if that was her, she chose not to come out.

I escorted the three into the office, where Gloria took the same Queen Anne chair she'd used before. Judith and Avery sat near the desk, with Hobbes across from them, glaring.

"Well?" Judith crossed her arms, frigid eyes meeting glare with glare.

"Miss Borden, I have one question for you. Why did you not tell us of your connection to Meridian?"

"You were hired to prove whether or not my sister is a fraud, nothing more. Past history is irrelevant."

"Nonsense. Such proof would require extensive research. If she is deluded, the source of the delusion must be found, and none exists in Chicago. There is also the murder of Gladys Jones, which appears to be a result of this investigation. That alone should encourage you to cooperate."

She sighed. "Very well. That vile reporter, Wilder, from the *National Echo,* and his equally vile girlfriend, came to our house Thursday morning. Very early Thursday morning, the day of Gladys' wake, and asked a lot of ridiculous questions. They angered me, but Gloria took pleasure in their company, as she does with all fools and innocents; she persuaded me to go to my room and allow her to handle them. Your questions can't be much worse than theirs."

"I'll start with this one. In which house on River Street did you live?"

"Which house?" The question seemed to surprise her.

Before Hobbes could respond, the doorbell rang. He nodded to me, and I went to the front door. It was Richie Butler; I realized for the first time that he and his dad hadn't started their work in the basement that morning. Richie had dark rings around his eyes, and his voice trembled as he asked, "Please, Abel, may I see Mr. Hobbes? My dad sent me."

I took him to the office, and he stopped just inside the door.

Hobbes saw the distress in the boy's face, and asked gently, "What is it, Richie?"

"Dad's in the hospital," he said, his voice catching. "He had a heart attack early this morning. The paramedics got there in time, and he's gonna be all right, but he wanted me to come by and let you know."

"When you see him again, Richie, tell him we wish him well."

"Thank you Mr. Hobbes, but that isn't all. He said to tell you it would be a couple of months before he could tear the cistern out, and maybe you didn't need to do that anyway. He said that instead of an elevator, you could have someone put a chair lift in the stairway, and it would save you a lot of money."

"Tell him not to worry, son. We'll talk to him when he gets home."

"And they can take the bricks and mortar back, if you want them to." That seemed to be all he had to say, for he lowered his head, turned and left.

Hobbes said to no one in particular, "Some men have a deeper sense of responsibility than others."

He returned his attention to Judith. "Please continue, madam."

Instead of answering, she turned a questioning glance at Avery. He cleared his throat and said, "We need a brief conference." Then, he and Judith went to talk to Gloria.

A moment later, they returned to the desk, but didn't sit back down.

"We have changed our minds," Avery said. "In view of Gladys' death, Cassius will probably drop his claim, and we will have indirectly solved our problem. Your commission is now considered complete and your fee earned. Upon receipt of your expense statement, a check for the contracted amount, plus expenses, will be issued." He smiled and showed a lot of teeth — shark's teeth. "Consider your services terminated. You no longer have a client."

Hobbes' long, narrow face turned stony, but I could hear his teeth grinding together. Or maybe those were mine. I looked into each face, but could see no compromise, only relief. Even Gloria's usually bemused expression was changed somehow.

My boss's only comment was, "What about Gladys' murderer?"

Someone answered, "Chicago's police are adequate." They marched out of the house in tandem. A few minutes later, I heard the limo drive away. I also heard Hobbes use an expression he seldom used.

After a while, he sighed. "They came here assuming I knew which house had been theirs. Without that knowledge, I have nothing to give the police. Bad judgment to ask that question first."

"What do we do now, chief?"

"Now?" He slid his fingers down his moustache, and smiled slightly. "We've been fired. We call Sally and Fred, and tell them to come home."

A while later, Cassius drove up in a six-year-old Buick — he didn't seem to live exorbitantly, and greeted Hobbes with an apology. "Avery called me on the car phone. Too bad. But it's their decision."

"I no longer have the right to ask questions on their behalf," Hobbes said. "But if I did, I would ask which house had been your former residence."

"I'd tell you if I could," was the reply, "But it has to do with family honor. Sorry, but I think even Gladys would agree. Some secrets we cannot voluntarily give away."

"Yet, one of you murdered Gladys."

"I know that's what you and Abel think, Car'l, but it may have been an outsider. Getting in wouldn't have been much of a problem, and a lot of people know about the passageways. She may have just surprised a burglar. Something simple as that." Rarely had anyone called the boss by his first name, unless invited to. I was surprised, but the familiarity seemed to suit Cassius. At any rate, Hobbes ignored it.

"And the disappearance of the pictures?"

"Who knows? But it doesn't have to be connected to the killer." The fact was, Hobbes and I knew, he could be right. Assumptions built on coincidence were the basis of many paranormal beliefs. They were exactly the sorts of things we tried to disprove, and it shouldn't be any different in the world of murder. That didn't mean he *was* right.

Marilyn came shortly after her father had left. Avery had called her too, she said, so her visit had become social, not business. My heart wasn't really in it, but I took her down to the boathouse and introduced her to Charon, pointing out that he was the boatman.

"Where are the boats, Mr. Charon?" she asked.

"Over there." He pointed to the rowboat.

"That's all?"

"Mr. Hobbes doesn't go out on the river much. Tell you what, though, you and young Houston come by after dark, and I'll take you out for a romantic boat ride."

She looked at the rowboat, then at me. "If I'm still here, perhaps we will."

We walked along the river, talking, but she was cautious about what she said. She did tell me a few things that I hadn't known, not that they mattered since we weren't on the case anymore. She said her aunts had changed the story of Eldred — the name had been chosen by Gloria — over the years, that Aunt Gloria and a man of that name had once had a mad love affair. One day he just disappeared and she never got over him. His ghost was invented, Marilyn supposed, to keep him real to her.

Sometime that afternoon I mentioned Kirk, the treasury man, and the counterfeiting. I expected her to laugh at the coincidence of names, but she didn't. Instead, she became introspective. "That's not so far-fetched as you might think. Did you notice the paintings at the house? Especially the two landscapes by Monet?" I shook my head. "Master replicas," she said. "Both of them. It would take an expert to tell they weren't the originals, except for one small detail. A conceit of the painter that proves it's only a copy."

"That being...?"

"If you looked at the crossing of the 't' in 'Monet,' with a magnifying glass, you wouldn't see a simple brush stroke."

"I'd see the name 'Eldred,'" I said, finishing her sentence.

"Right, and every painting in that house was done by him. Aunt Gloria brought them with her when they moved in from, I guess now, from Meridian."

That wouldn't explain fake money made after his death. But if he were still alive, where was he?

She apologized for not seeing me at the wake. She had known what it would be like when the Gloria worshippers came, she said, so she had gone to the chapel earlier that afternoon and cried her goodbyes alone.

Later that night, we floated gently on the river; the soft stroke of Charon's oars slipping through the water playing a quiet serenade for lovers.

Chapter 25

Monday. It was only our third Monday on the case but it had seemed like forever, Hobbes sent a registered letter detailing his expenses to the Bordens. Tuesday, he talked to his lawyer about filing a civil suit against the *Echo* and Tom Wilder, but the lawyer advised waiting until Wilder made an appearance; he hadn't been seen since the day he had talked Hobbes into sending me to the *Echo*. Thursday, a cashier's check drawn on the Madison Bank of Chicago came, closing the case. In the meantime, the house was quiet as a tomb, its living bodies interred. Anger and frustration vied with remorse and resignation until Friday morning, when resignation seemed to win out.

"The least we can do for Gladys," Hobbes said, "is to take her some flowers. Sally will show you where the grave is, Abel. The nature of the remembrance I leave to you."

Take some flowers, he had said, not *send* some flowers. I looked for some hidden meaning in that curious request, but as usual, he was inscrutable.

An hour later, I placed a spray of roses and carnations across the fresh grave, and whispered, "We haven't given up yet, Gladys." It wasn't till after a minute of reflection that I looked at the other headstones in that family plot.

The last name on all of them was "Kelly."

As in Gladys *Kelly* Jones.

We were back in business.

As Sally and I drove back to the house on River Street, I wondered if Hobbes could have known what I'd find, and if so, how did he know? The *Kelly* name on those tombstones had caught me completely off guard, and I thought I'd known as much about the case as he did. Hobbes sometimes seemed almost supernatural, which was kind of odd for a person who didn't believe in such.

He gave us a rare smile when I told him, and said, "Excellent." He leaned back in his wheelchair, laced his fingers together across his belly, and allowed his eyes to droop nearly shut. Had he been able to, he would have put his feet on the desk.

"I've been thinking, Abel, Sally. Now that we have completed our contractual obligation to the Bordens and have been compensated, we are free to honor the pledge I made to Gladys at her wake." For Sally's benefit, he added, "I promised to find her killer and bring that person to justice."

Sally had been sad ever since she saw the cut flowers I'd bought for Gladys, but the prospect of righting some wrong brought color to her face, and she responded with an enthusiastic, "Very good, sir."

"I shall consider Gladys Jones to be my client, and the fee will be the pictures she promised to you, Abel, which you would have brought to me. That may not be as legal as a written contract, but it will be adequate for the short time I expect this investigation to last. Do you find this agreeable?"

"Sounds good to me. Do you want me to get Fred's opinion?"

Hobbes opened his eyes slightly. "He has already concurred."

So the boss had been pretty sure I'd find something. I asked him, "Did you already know about the names on the graves?"

"It was a possibility. You knew Gladys. Did you think of her as an old maid?"

"I'm sure she was."

"You thought that because you had met her and formed that opinion early. When you called the police that night, you said she was 'Gladys Kelly Jones,' as if 'Kelly' was her middle name. When you later repeated it to me, 'Kelly' sounded like a maiden name, although I didn't know she had never married. Last night I wondered, why would she prearrange to spend eternity with strangers? Perhaps 'Jones' had been added to give her some anonymity when she moved to Chicago, and perhaps death dispelled that need for secrecy."

"So, you had me take some flowers to the gravesite, figuring I'd see something as obvious as names on tombstones." Obvious. Yeah.

"Sally," he said, changing the subject. "You mentioned a priest at the grave. Priests have churches; churches keep records of births, baptisms and christenings. Find the priest and his church so that you can search those records; it should be sufficient to limit your search to the years between nineteen-thirty-five and forty."

"I know the priest," she said, smiling. My guess was that she knew which church, too.

He turned his attention to me. "There are more than a score of Kellys listed in the phone book. One or two of them may have information about Gladys. There were no Bordens."

"Right, boss. I'll use the phone in the kitchen"; my stomach was telling me that it was lunchtime. There was some leftover something from last night in the fridge. He was reaching for his own telephone before I was out of the room.

As I ate, I tried to decide on the best approach. Telling a complete stranger I was investigating a murder would turn on all sorts of internal alarms, and probably scare him, or her, into silence. On the other hand, if I hinted at the possibility of inheriting some money, he or she would very likely answer at least the basic questions, and for now, that was all I wanted.

My first call was answered on the second ring.

"Kelly here."

"Good afternoon, sir. Am I talking to Mr. Allen Kelly?"

"Depends on whether you're trying to collect alimony for my ex-wife."

I laughed politely. "Oh no, not me. I'm not after money."

"Then I'm Allen. Tell you a secret, though, I don't have an ex trying to get my money. Got something worse. Two kids in college. Ha, ha. It's a joke, boy. Now what can I do for you?"

"My name is Abel Houston," I began. "I've been retained to find surviving relatives of Gladys Jones, whose maiden name was Kelly. She lived in this area until about forty years ago, when she was twenty-one or so, then moved to Chicago. Does she sound like someone you'd be related to?"

"Name sounds familiar. Was she the woman that was killed in that fortune teller's house in Chicago?"

"Yes," I said. "A lousy way to die."

"I read about it in the *Echo*. My wife picks it up. Wouldn't waste money on those tabloids, myself. But to answer your question, we've only lived here four years. Don't even know any other Kellys."

I thanked him, and hung up.

Except for three no-answers and the two picked up by answering machines — all of which I'd try again later — calls two through twenty-two yielded essentially the same results. Not that everyone was positive they weren't related, but forty years is a long time.

Sally's luck had been better. She had not only found the priest, but also the record of Gladys' christening, which included the names of her parents and godparents. Father Burr said the mother was still living, and he visited her often at the nursing home. She still had her mental faculties, he said, but her memory wasn't as sharp as it used to be. As far as he knew, she had no relatives, at least none that visited her.

Sally had gone to the nursing home and spent an hour with Mrs. Lucille Kelly. Fred and I were with Hobbes when she made her report.

"She thinks she's seventy-two," Sally said, "But her records say she is eighty-nine. That makes the accuracy of her recollections suspect, but I think what she told me is basically correct."

During the next ten minutes, Sally summarized the interview. In the hour and a half that followed, she repeated what had been said almost word for word. Hobbes questioned her, asking about her impressions and about the subtle evasions that Mrs. Kelly might have unknowingly used while talking to Sally — if she had secrets relevant to our investigation. A few initial remarks were interesting, and one or two were surprising.

"She and Gladys hadn't gotten along," Sally reported. "She had completely planned the girl's future. Her school, boyfriends, college, even named a potential husband. According to Lucy, Gladys rebelled. Didn't appreciate any of her sacrifices, she said, and she'd scrimped and saved for that ungrateful child. When she was sixteen, Gladys left home, and went to work for those uppity sisters who lived alone, except for their kid brother, on River Street. Went to work as a *housekeeper*. Just to be near that boy, that *Cash*." She paused and watched Hobbes for his reaction.

He nodded and brought his hand up, saluting her.

She continued, "I don't know if Gladys and Cassius were lovers, but Lucy thought they were. Anyway, the mother and daughter didn't talk for five years, and then Gladys disappeared."

He turned to me. "Is there a chance that Marilyn is a result of their continued union?"

I shook my head. "It's my opinion there was never a first union."

He went back to Sally. "Did she mention other names? Last names?"

"She was pretty resentful about a 'Judith,' who took advantage of her poor daughter, underpaying and overworking her. And there was a man called Avery who also lusted after Gladys, but she didn't remember any last names."

I tried to picture Avery lusting after Gladys and shook my head. No. I couldn't imagine any man, ever, lusting after Gladys.

After Hobbes finished his cross-examination of Sally, he leaned back and thoughtfully stroked the ends of his moustache. "We seem to face a conspiracy of aliases and forgotten names. Perhaps it's time to change our approach."

"Now yer talking," Fred said. "Start looking fer people instead of names."

Hobbes looked at the fireman with respect. "Exactly. We can narrow the time period to the years before the Bordens left Meridian. The place we can limit to River Street. And the people we'll be concerned about are twin girls, who were then about thirty five years old, and a man named Eldred, who disappeared.

"Sally, I suggest the microfilm records of the newspapers of that period at the community college. Letters to the editor, society pages, the police blotter. You know better than I where to look and what to look for.

"Fred, many of your cronies still visit the VFW or the Legion Hall, or they may follow the euchre circuit. Some of them will have clear memories of things that happened long ago. Perhaps you would have some success in getting them to recall interesting rumors of that period."

He paused before giving me my assignment, a puzzled look on his face. Finally he said, slowly, "I'm uncertain of your status, Abel. I feel we're missing something."

"Chief?"

"Bullets were fired in your direction. They were obviously a warning, but from whom? A street gang? If so, there is no further danger as long as you stay away from that part of the city. But if the warning came from someone engaged by the murderer, then why was it sent? Do you know something you were not then aware of that may yet endanger your life?"

"You know everything I know."

"Perhaps. Yet it may be something so mundane you barely noticed, but which the murderer feels is of great importance."

I shrugged. "Not a clue."

"Then what I'd like you to do, Abel, is to review everything that happened up there before the shooting. Take a day or two and use your mind's eye to view each event, each place, from every angle you can think of. Concentrate on the commonplace. Remember this. If you were in danger once, then you may face an imminent and more deadly danger as we close in on the killer.

"Now," he said, his voice suddenly cheerful, "If someone will bring the Town Car around, I'll spring for supper. Red Lobster, or Ruby Tuesday's. Anyplace, as long as it has a bar. I'm hungry *and* thirsty, and there are new beers I'd like to try."

We went instead to *La Plume de Ma Tante.* Despite the French-sounding name, which I thought might mean 'My Aunt's Pen,' it was not French, nor even foreign. It was, however, a three-star restaurant. It was also expensive for a small town like Meridian, drawing most of its customers from out of town. Some came for the food, but others came to see the mural that filled most of the forty-foot long eastern wall. The mural had been a work in progress for over two years. It was an artist's version of the history of space exploration. It began with Sputnik, then progressed through the Apollo missions, the moon landing, the shuttles, and was finishing with a space station. *I might have been a part of that,* I thought wistfully. Still, I was glad for those who had been there.

I almost bumped into the last woman I'd ever want to bump into, but I caught myself at the last second. Our waitress led us to a table across the room. I tried to be inconspicuous by sitting with my back to that woman, but positioning myself to still see her in the mirrors behind our table.

A minute later, I watched her sit down with the Butlers. A young man was with her that I recognized as her son, Luke Ransom. I wondered how much Katya knew about space and the space missions. I guessed it to be quite a bit, judging from the animated way she was talking.

We could have ordered caviar or lobster, I suppose, but we managed to do justice to two bottles of decent Champagne and about a quarter of a cow. I really didn't have room for much else, but I looked at the desert menu anyway. One thing stood out from all the rest, and I showed it to Hobbes. *Tapioca ala Fred.*

"Strange things happen in Meridian," he murmured.

"Any fool could see that!" We all looked up, and it was her; Katya Ransom had found us. "No, don't bother to stand up," She let the corners of her mouth droop in a kind of sardonic smile. "They call you a cripple, but I know better. You're as phony as that Borden tramp!"

Chapter 26

Hobbes spun his chair around to face Katya; he tilted his head slightly. "You honor me. I wish you were as good a judge of people as you think you are. I would trade my reputation for a pair of working legs any time."

"Liar," she said, and turned to me. "And you. You wanted to be an astronaut, didn't you? But you sure screwed that up. Claustrophobia? Hah! Put your head in a box; that'll cure it." She paused for a second, then added, "They should have sent you to space, anyway. Just think, at this very moment, you could be gasping for breath on some airless planet like Neptune, or maybe crashed on one of its frozen moons."

"Mother, please." Luke Ransom, took her arm, and nodded to us. "You'll have to excuse her. We were just out for supper, same as you. Then, she said she saw Hobbes and Houston and had to go talk to them. She doesn't mean anything." He led her away without waiting for a response.

"The hell she didn't," Fred growled.

Something she had said nagged at me, but I couldn't quite figure out what it was. It seemed important, and I tried to bring it out, but all I could do was shake my head and wait. Maybe later.

"She doesn't like you very much," Sally said, and laughed.

After we returned from supper, Fred said there were a couple of hours left before the old timers went off to bed, and he might as well get going. Sally said she'd start early tomorrow, and sat down to watch a little TV. I went to my room, turned on my stereo, and tried to let Beethoven stimulate my memory. I started my review at the moment Gladys first greeted me and followed it through to the point where Cassius loaned me the *Bull's* cap. Nothing. I went backwards from the end to the beginning, like a film running in reverse. I tried freeze frame, slow motion, and fast forward. I visualized scenes from other people's points of view. Still nothing.

What was it Katya Ransom had said?

I brushed my teeth, turned off the stereo and the lights, and went to bed. This time, it took three minutes to get to sleep. The case was making me an insomniac.

When I woke up Saturday morning, it was with the feeling that Hobbes was right. There was something I'd seen, casually, while I had been involved with something else of more immediate importance. An impression floated obliquely around the edges of my mind, teasing with obscure hints that I couldn't quite focus upon. It was like trying to put a name to a face you'd seen briefly at a New Year's Eve party, without being sure of the face, or even sure it was worth remembering. I knew I had Katya to thank for that, whatever it was.

I went down to the kitchen and poured a cup of coffee. As I searched the cabinets for something to eat, I decided to let my subconscious work it out. When it was ready for me, I'd know. I settled for *Lucky Charms* and grapefruit juice — there wasn't a lot to choose from.

After my meager breakfast, I reviewed the videotapes of the séance and let the images flow without questioning anything. Then, I went outside and sat in the front seat of the Town Car and visualized the circle drive in back of the house on Belleview. If Sally's Bronco had been around, I'd have sat in it, too. Nothing.

Inside again, I called Marilyn and talked to her for an hour. I said we had a new client — her name was "Kelly," and would she, Marilyn, like to come down and go for another boat ride? She said she'd love to, and would after dark be all right? And was it "Kelly" as in "Gladys Kelly Jones?" I said she'd make a great paranormal snoop, and we both laughed more than we needed to.

Fred came in about four-thirty. "Talk to you and Hobbes when Sally gets home. Got the lowdown fer his nibs and the hired help." He winked at me, "I been cooking with gas all day, and I'm gonna cook with gas fer supper. Gonna broil salmon in butter sauce and bake potatoes. What do you think about that?"

All I could think to say was, "Be careful." At six o'clock, Hobbes and I joined him for the first home-cooked meal the kitchen had seen in months. We ate in silent grateful surprise.

Sally came home about seven, her eyes glowing. "Come with me, guys. Breakthrough!" She put her hands above her head and did a pirouette. "Wait'll you hear what I've got for Hobbes."

"It can wait fifteen minutes," I said. "First you gotta see what Fred's got for *you*."

Eager to talk to the boss, but sidetracked by curiosity, she followed me into the kitchen. She stared wide-eyed as Fred took the supper he'd been keeping warm for her from the oven and put it on the table.

A half hour later, we pulled upholstered chairs around Hobbes' desk, and made ourselves comfortable. Fred told Sally to go first.

She stood up, bowed deeply to the rest of us, said, "Thank you, sirs, each of you," and sat back down.

"As Mr. Hobbes suggested," she began, "I went to the community college and searched the microfilm copies of the local newspaper, starting with the first day of summer, forty years ago. The issue dated July twenty-three, nineteen fifty-seven, had this." She handed each of us a photocopy of an article.

"Local Woman Cheated," the story read. "Mrs. Irene Fox, who lives on Orson Boulevard in Meridian, complained to the police that she was cheated out of three hundred dollars by a man who was to buy new bricks and repair her fireplace. The man, Eldred Brown, whose name the police believe is false, disappeared the day he was given the money." She looked at each of us and smiled brightly.

"How many Eldreds who laid bricks do you suppose there are?" She asked.

"Anyway, I checked the phone book to see if anyone named Fox still lived on Orson, and there was one, listed as Fox, comma, E. It was worth a phone call.

"A woman answered; I told her I was trying to find an Irene Fox who may have lived there forty years ago. She said Irene was her mother, but she'd died in 'seventy-five. Why was I looking for her?

"I told her that I was trying to find out about Eldred Brown who was said to have cheated her mother, and asked if she knew anything about him. There was a long silence when I thought she was going to hang up. Instead she said, 'Do I? Listen, there's something I've wanted to talk about for a long time. Do you have an hour to spare?'

"Did I?" Sally paused a moment to pour herself some water from the pitcher on Hobbes' desk, and took a sip. "I was there in fifteen minutes.

"She was a large woman, about seventy. She introduced herself as Ellen and asked me to come in. She was a retired school teacher, she said, and had devoted her life to her career. Only once had she found time for a man. That was when Eldred showed up.

"'He was a curious man,' she told me. 'He learned bricklaying from his father, but I don't think he was very good at it. Not like he said his brother was. His real talent lay somewhere else. He was an artist.'

"Ellen had me sit by the coffee table and drink iced tea. She opened an old flat box and showed me some drawings he had sketched of her and for her. Even though they had been done quickly, and in charcoal, they showed her with beauty and passion.

"'I think I was in love,' she told me. 'I celebrated his thirty-seventh birthday with him. July eighteenth. I remember it well. He said he loved me, too. He said he had been born near me, and he wanted to die near me. Five days later he disappeared forever.'"

Sally sighed deeply. She enjoyed sad, melancholy stories. "There's a lot more, but I don't think it's important to the case." She took a picture from her purse and placed it face down on the desk in front of Hobbes. "This is."

He turned the photograph over and studied it for a long moment, then handed it to Fred. The fireman sucked in a deep breath, then expelled it like it was poisonous smoke. He held the picture out to me. It was four decades old, but the face was unmistakable.

"Avery!" I said. Avery pretending to be Eldred? Why?

"Ellen told me I could keep this. She has a lot more." Sally's voice was soft, as if she was making it fit the melancholy of the story.

"If the dates are right, he would have been born July eighteen, nineteen twenty," Hobbes said, after a moment of mental arithmetic. "If his birth was near here, the record should be available in the county clerk's office. A search of that day for an Eldred should not be difficult."

"First thing Monday morning."

Hobbes glanced at Fred. It was his turn.

"Ain't got nothin' new, like Sally," he said, light from the desk lamps bouncing off his shining head. "What I got goes back real far, maybe sixty years.

"Took a lot of talking, a lot of beers. And a lot of trips out back to see a man about a horse." He chuckled at his old-timer's euphemism for going to the restroom and went on. "Was out till two this morning and didn't get nowhere. About noon today, though, a

World War Two vet got to talking about how things were before he went into the army, back around 'thirty-seven or thirty-eight. There were these twin girls he was interested in. Pretty little things, he said, but their folks thought they was upper crust. Wouldn't let the likes of him close. Then he took a drink, and laughed before telling me that justice was served in its own way. One of the girls left town with her mother. To stay with an aunt in Galena, he recollected. When they came back six months later, she had a 'baby brother.' He looked at me, real serious, 'The girl's mother was almost fifty, what d'you think? Some people do anything to keep the family name pure, right?' I agreed, and asked if he remembered their names.

"'Never forgot 'em,' he says. 'They was too pretty to forget. Lived on River Street. Gloria and Judith Albany.' Then he looked around the room a little, and told me, 'Card game's about to start and my partner's lookin' at me, so I oughta get over there. Tell you what, though, you come back tomorrow, we'll have a couple beers, and I'll show you where they lived.'"

Hobbes looked at Fred, then at Sally, and tilted his head forward. "I salute you both," he said. "We have knowledge undreamed of forty-eight hours ago. Who knows what the morrow will bring." He turned his attention to me: "Abel, I continue to feel something is missing."

"So do I. It's buzzing around in my head somewhere, but it's staying just out of reach."

"I urge you to take extra care, then. I do not believe in precognition, but I still sense danger."

"Here?" I asked.

He considered the question for a moment, but before he could answer, the doorbell rang and I went to answer it. It was Marilyn. We had a date with a boat.

I had talked to Charon earlier, and he'd said we could take the rowboat out ourselves, so long as we wore our life vests. If it got too cool, there was a blanket under the seat.

"If you go ashore anywhere, them mosquitoes are gonna eat you alive," was his final warning.

It was after eleven when we pushed off with beer and sandwiches in a cooler; the moon was shining brightly, shimmering across the slow moving water. I rowed up river for about ten minutes and grounded the boat under an old oak tree that leaned comfortably out over the water.

We pulled the boat up onto the shore and spread the blanket on the sandy grass. The mosquitoes didn't waste any time finding us, but I had listened to Charon and brought along some citronella candles.

Up to that time, I hadn't known how beautiful a woman could become, the deeper the attraction went. It wasn't the moonlight, or the candlelight, or the soft summer breeze that came gently across the river that changed her. It was something else. I thought about it as I lay back on the blanket and gazed at the moon.

She sat down close to me, and for a few seconds I tried to put a name to her perfume, but decided that wasn't very important at the moment.

"You know what this reminds me of, Abel?" she said in a sort of faraway voice.

"Gilligan's Island?"

'Nothing like that."

"Spring break your third year in college?"

"Don't be silly. Students of anthropology never had time for that sort of thing. No, it was my third summer in graduate school and half a dozen of us had gone to the Amazon rain forest somewhere in Brazil. We were supposed to study a primitive tribe that had built a village very close to the Amazon River. We made a camp nearby and had just settled in for the first night, when we were attacked by ferocious alligators. Or was it crocodiles, I can never remember which."

"Uh huh," I said.

"We were rescued by a wandering band of gorillas that carried us off into the trees, like Tarzan and Jane."

"Is that a fact?"

"Oh, don't sound so skeptical," she said. "Besides, the biggest and strongest ape looked just like you."

I turned on my side and studied her. "Then what happened?"

"I'll have to show you," she said.

She attacked me. Sort of.

And I defended myself. Sort of.

Four or five hours later, with the eastern sky graying, we rowed back. Halfway across, I realized I was thinking whimsical thoughts, like marriage, and children. After we put the boat back in the boathouse,

I said it was late for her to be driving sixty miles back home, and mentioned that we had a spare bedroom. I could see her smile in the moonlight, but she said no, people might talk.

We shared a long quiet moment outside her car, then she got in, started the engine, waved at me, and backed out of the driveway.

Chapter 27

As I walked back toward the house, I noticed a light in the basement and wondered if Clyde Butler had left it on, when, a week ago? Could be. Hardly anyone ever went down there. Had he even locked the inside cellar doors after they had unloaded the bricks?

To my surprise, the door to the basement was open. Anybody could get in. I should have checked it long ago. I went in and closed the door behind me, turning the deadbolt. There. Safe again. I went to the stairs, intending to go up to the main floor, and turn the lights off from there, but I was stopped by a noise — a skittering sound, like a big mouse running across the floor. I listened and heard it again. It was somewhere around the cistern.

I followed the noise, more curious every moment. It didn't really *sound* like a mouse. What was it? It seemed like it was coming from inside the cistern. I stuck my head through the rough doorway that had been made years ago when they had quit using the cistern; I heard it again. As my eyes adjusted to the darkness, I finally saw it rolling across the floor. A ping-pong ball. A *ping-pong ball?*

I heard a soft step behind me, followed by a sharp whack. Incredible pain raced up my back to the base of my skull, and my legs gave out. I fell, slipping into darkness. A coarse whisper followed me down. *"You should have heeded the warning. Why didn't you leave us alone?"*

Space is time. Gravity warps space. Black holes suck up nebulae. Stars appear and fade away. I was a part of them all, and then I wasn't. I was an astronaut. Then I was afraid and then I wasn't. I heard the ripping of duck tape and felt it going around my wrists, and my legs, and my mouth. I faded out. I was eclipsed.

I came back for just a moment. Vaguely, I heard the sound of harsh, rapid breathing. Hands jerked me across the rough floor, a little at a time. And something warm and wet was on the back of my neck — wet but drying. Then I was with Buzz in the Lunar Rover, and it was going plop, swish, swish. Softly, quietly, secretly, plop, swish, swish.

Wait a minute. The moon was airless, you couldn't hear on the moon. Plop, swish, swish. I came back to earth and opened my eyes. Someone was building a wall of bricks — plop, some mortar going down — swish, swish, smooth it with a trowel — lay a brick — plop, some mortar going down, and up and up goes the cockeyed wall, uneven and unaligned — or was that me? I could see light, but the bricks were almost to the ceiling, and I was fading.

I thought I heard the upstairs door open, and footsteps on the stairs. The stairs were above me. The footsteps came to my level and walked past me. A voice, a boy's voice, said triumphantly, "*Yes! Got it.*" Then the footsteps started back toward the stairs. I called to him. "Over here," I said, but he couldn't hear me. My mouth was taped. I tried to make a noise with my feet, but I couldn't move. I moaned. The footsteps stopped. A second later, I heard something drop to the floor. Then I heard the boy running up the stairs, yelling, "Mr. Hobbes! Mr. Hobbes!" Finally I heard the deadbolt being unlocked, and the basement door open, and then close.

I was back in space. There was darkness around me. No stars. A distant light formed at the end of a tunnel. I could hear hammering and the falling of bricks. I felt hands pull the tape off my mouth. I saw the light coming for me, white and warm and inviting. I was dying. Hobbes should see this, I thought.

Then there was nothing.

* * * * *

I was near the planet Neptune, about 3 billion miles from home. I was fascinated by one of her icy moons. In my dream, it was bright and glowing, until it disappeared into the shadow of the planet — as if it had been switched off. It reminded me of what Katya Ransom had said about a frozen moon, and suddenly my fumbling mind put things together and I knew what it meant. Then a strange voice said, "Would you move to your left a little, Miss Borden. I can't see the monitor."

The moon came back, and I wanted to tell Hobbes about it, so I left the eighth planet and returned to earth. "He's coming around," the stranger said. The room came into focus.

A voice more familiar spoke up. "Marilyn, I think his hand will be all right now." She reluctantly let go, and moved out of the way. Hobbes rolled close to the bed. "How's your head?"

"Vibrating." I remembered the basement. "How am I?"

"Concussion, shock, bad cut on the back of your head. Out for half a day."

I groaned. "I don't suppose you know who did it."

"We hoped you knew."

I shook my head. "But I remembered something." I motioned for him to lean down and whispered, "The moon was Triton."

"Moon?"

"Yeah. You can see it sometime, but it can go out like this." I tried to snap my fingers. "Trust me. You can bank on that." I was rambling, talking in code. What kind of pain killing stuff did the hospital have me on? Or was I talking like that because there was a cop in the room, and he had leaned down with Hobbes so he could hear what I said? I saw the boss's brief nod of acknowledgement. I figured if he wanted to tell the local police about the people up north, it was up to him.

The policeman was courteous and reasonably thorough, and formed the preliminary theory of a nutcase burglar. One who stumbled upon bricks and mortar and thought it might be fun to use them. Since it was attempted murder, they were going over the crime scene for prints and such, as well as talking to the neighbors. He'd keep us posted, he promised, and left me to rest. I was surprised by how tired I was, and how easy it was to fall back to sleep.

When I woke up again, Hobbes and Marilyn had left. Richie Butler and Fred had taken their places. I was not surprised that Sally had not come. I don't think Sally would ever come to a hospital by choice. It had been Richie who had heard me in the basement and had brought help. I managed to raise myself to my elbows and said, "Thanks, Rich." Calling him "Richie" didn't seem appropriate any more. That was a juvenile nickname, and he'd been man enough to save my life.

He shook his head. "Huh-uh. It was Mr. Hobbes. You shoulda seen him. He scooted down the stairs on his butt like a little kid and had me bring the wheelchair. Then, he wheeled around the stairs and saw the bricks. 'Get Fred out of bed and call emergency,' he said. I ran upstairs and beat on Fred's door and yelled at him what had happened. He came running out with his ax and headed for the stairs while I grabbed a phone. When I got down there, Mr. Hobbes was swinging the ax from his wheels, cracking the bricks loose, and Fred was stacking them on the floor so they wouldn't fall in on you. By the time the EMT's arrived, we'd opened up a hole big enough to get you out. With that blood and everything, you really looked bad, Abel. I thought you might be dead." He grinned suddenly, and added, "But you kept saying, 'let me sleep.'"

The fireman grunted in agreement, but didn't comment.

"Wasn't that pretty early in the morning for you to come over?" I was still trying to put things together.

"Seven on a Sunday morning? Hah! You know Dad. *He's* under doctor's orders to take it easy for a while, but I'm not. He wanted me to level our pool table, and as soon as he thought someone was up at your house, he sent me over to get his tools." He paused. "Lucky, I guess. An hour later, and, well... I might not have heard you."

Lucky? I wondered. Hobbes didn't believe in luck, or in divine providence either. What would he call this? Well, we didn't agree on everything.

"Mr. Hobbes wants me to come back tomorrow and clean up the basement." The boy seemed uncertain and eager at the same time. The police would be gone; would there still be clues?

"Let me know if you find anything, Rich," I said.

He told me he'd better get going. He'd left his old bike chained to a handicapped parking sign, he said, and he didn't have a handicapped parking card.

I spent a while talking to Fred, who said Hobbes and Marilyn had gone out for supper, then I gradually dropped back off to sleep.

The hospital released me around noon Tuesday with the standard instructions; take it easy and rest, Tylenol for headache, see your own doctor. I could see Fred had news as he drove me home, but he wouldn't tell me what. Said the boss was waiting for Sally to report.

He went out of his way to stop at a KFC for a bucket of chicken, potatoes and gravy, and coleslaw.

Hobbes said he was waiting for Sally to confirm some details, so I ate an impatient lunch at the kitchen table with him, Fred, and surprisingly, Rich.

Something was happening, and everyone seemed to know about it but me. No one would talk — at least not about the case. Fred wondered if the

Chicago Bears would make it to the Super Bowl, and Hobbes said they had two chances, fat and slim. Fred then asked if anyone wanted to watch a John Wayne video with him, and fifteen-year-old Rich said, John *Who?* I got up in disgust and went to the library to read a book.

At half past four, Sally stepped in and said the boss wanted us all in the office. She said it quietly, but her eyes glittered. When I stood up, she took my arms and waltzed me to the door. "Hobbes is pleased," she said.

Four chairs formed a half circle around the sides and front of Hobbes' desk with Hobbes behind it. He had Sally sit in the first chair to his right. Fred was next to her, in front. Then Rich, also in front of the desk, and finally me at the boss's left, where I could see everyone.

As he looked us over, he leaned back in his wheelchair and caressed the wheel rails with his hands. "The tide has changed," he said. "That it has done so is in no small measure due to young Richard Butler. I think we all agree he has earned himself a seat in this meeting. Not only for saving Abel's life, but for information he provided me earlier today."

Hobbes turned to me. "Actually, Sally, Fred, and Richard have all discovered things yesterday and this morning that you don't know, Abel. I have asked them to repeat it all for you, to see if you reach the same conclusions as I did."

I grinned. Hobbes *knew*. He had it all figured out. It was all done except for fitting the iron bracelets. So to speak.

Like Hobbes, I leaned back in my chair. "You have my full attention, Boss."

"Sally will begin with background details, Fred will focus them on a specific area, and Richard will bring us home." He nodded to his right. "If you will, Sally?"

All eyes turned to the cemetery girl.

She nodded. "I was at the County Clerk's office when it opened yesterday. It wasn't hard to find the names of everyone born on July eighteenth, nineteen twenty. There was only one Eldred, and his last name was not Carpunky. He was a son of John and Edith Stone. I discovered later that the Stones operated a brickyard until they retired in nineteen sixty. They were an established family, and a lot of people were willing to talk about them. For example, they said Eldred was a gifted artist who hated having to work in the brickyard to earn a living. Working for his father, who barely tolerated him. Those seemed to be facts. The rumors were more interesting. Especially the one that said Eldred had gotten a girl pregnant, but no one knew who she was. Only that she left town, and everything was hushed up. Does that sound familiar?"

Hobbes applauded her. "A lot of information for a single morning, Sally. One question I'll ask for Abel's sake. The rest of us already know the answer. Did the Stones have any other children?"

She looked at me and answered gleefully, "Now that you mention it, they did. His name was Avery. He was born on that same day as Eldred. People talked about him too. They said he had no artistic talent but went to college and became a lawyer — a very good lawyer."

Twins. Another pair of twins. I supposed I should have been surprised, but somehow I wasn't. The picture of Eldred that Ellen Fox had given Sally suddenly made sense. No wonder we thought it was Avery.

"And after that, Sally?"

"I drove up to Galena last night, and this morning I went to their county courthouse. The record I looked for turned out exactly as you expected. Cassius Albany, born nineteen thirty-six. Mother, Gloria Albany. Father..." Sally loved pausing for dramatic effect. "Father, Eldred Stone."

Without hesitation, Hobbes switched to the fireman. "Your turn, Fred."

"Ain't much," was the answer. "Just that W.W.Two vet showing me the Albany house." He rubbed his hand across his bald head and grinned. He liked drama, too. "We're sittin' in it."

And what a welcome home party this was!

Hobbes looked at the boy. "Tell us your surprise, Richard."

"Well, I went to clean up the basement yesterday, and I guess I was kinda looking for clues. Anyway, the biggest thing I noticed was the way the cistern wall lined up with the stairs. It didn't look right. It looked thick, you know? If you looked at it just right. Especially after I cleaned out the area under the stairs where Abel was, you know, bricked in. I measured from the wall under the stairs to where the cistern wall is, and there's two feet unaccounted for."

He swallowed hard. "Abel, I don't think you were the first one. I think there's another crypt down there."

Chapter 28

Hobbes allowed me a moment to digest what I'd just heard, and to think about what might be in the basement below us; then he asked for my opinion.

"If you mean, do I know who killed Gladys, I can only say maybe."

"Will a visit to the basement help?"

"It might."

An hour later, Fred, Sally, and Rich had hammered down the second brick wall under the stairs while Hobbes and I watched. I was still too weak to help. The bricks were one-third the age of those that made up the foundation of the old house, but they had been poorly set and badly mortared. The wall came apart easily, giving way to the dry, musty smell of an ageless airtight tomb. When all but the lower eight or nine rows had been removed and stacked out of the way, Hobbes rolled his wheelchair around, and looked over the remaining wall, at what lay on the floor behind it. "The flashlight, Abel." I handed him one, and we watched over his shoulder.

The body wore blue denim jeans and a yellow and brown sport shirt. It lay chest down on the cement, but the head was twisted backward as if it was trying to see the unnatural cleavage where its spine should have been. The brown on the shirt was old blood. A hatchet lay at its feet.

The skin was dry and shriveled, drawn tight over the skull, pulled back from the teeth in a sardonic smile. The face was unmistakable. The corpse had long ago dried out and mummified, but it didn't look too much different from its living twin.

"I'm glad to meet you at last, Eldred Stone," Sally said quietly. "I've heard a lot about you. May you soon find rest."

Hobbes moved back out of the way. "Take out the rest of the bricks and give him some breathing room." I'm not sure if he was aware of the absurdity of his exact words, but I knew what he meant about room to breathe. Briefly, I wondered if the dead man had been claustrophobic, too. Not that it made any difference. He had been dead before he was interred. Like most people. I shivered and rephrased that last thought. Not everyone was dead before they were buried.

We didn't move the body any more than we had to. The police would not care for us to disturb the evidence. Still, we had to know. We had a *right* to know. I said, "Let me," and knelt by Eldred.

His clothes were rotting, but still intact, and I searched his pockets. What I found was almost too good to be true. Not just a billfold with identification in it, but an envelope, with pictures.

I stood up and handed them to Hobbes, and then we all looked over his shoulders — again — as he opened them. The ID said Eldred Stone, no surprise. The pictures might have been copies of the ones Gladys died for.

They were of the twins, both pairs of them. There was no sure way to tell the girls apart except that one frowned a lot. Guess who I thought that was. The men just looked identical; even in close–ups, there was nothing to distinguish them from each other.

The pictures had been taken at a birthday party, complete with cake with candles. We could probably count those with a magnifying glass. The four were horsing around and having fun; there was no indication of the identity of the photographer. In one picture, a man in a gray shirt had his arms around the smiling sister, holding her in a gentle embrace. In another, taken in front of the cellar door, a brother held an ax over the head of the other, who held up his hands in make-believe fear. A few more shots taken by moonlight showed the night-time beauty of the river and its reflection of the hospital clock.

"Put these things back with the body, Abel," Hobbes said. "We should call the police." He paused, and grimaced. "But another day won't matter. Not to the dead man, anyway." He turned to Rich. "The delay is illegal, and you are under age. You do not work for me and have no obligation to remain silent, although I believe that within twenty-four hours, I can reveal the murderer."

The boy grinned. "I was never down here, Mr. Hobbes."

"Thank you, Rich. Tomorrow, we'll contact the Bordens and Regasmun to tell them that we know identity of the murderer. We shall also tell them of our intentions to disclose the name, and the motive, to the police and to the press. The exposure will be at a two o'clock meeting whether or not they are here. Mr. Green will be invited to represent the press, and Lieutenant Murphy, the law."

"Murphy?" I wanted to be sure I heard right.

A Fine and Private Grave

"Murphy."

Chapter 29

Tuesday morning, the office was made ready.

Fred enlisted Rich as an associate furniture mover and rearranged Hobbes' living room/office. They left his desk at the west end, but moved both the blue and the gray sofas so they were close to the northeast and southeast corners of the desk, but angled so that Hobbes could see them equally well. One armchair was placed between them; another went to the right of the desk, and a third to its left. The remaining chairs, including the Queen Anne, were moved across the hall. A coffee table for the sofas, and a small table by each chair, completed the moves.

It was Hobbes' intention for everyone to sit in a specific arrangement, and he made it clear that he expected me to see to it. We excluded Fred, Sally, and Rich from the assigned seating. They would stay in the kitchen and listen to everything by way of the intercom. Charon, as always, chose to wander along the riverbank.

At one-fifteen, the doorbell rang. Forrest Green, our first guest, greeted me with a cheerful, "Abel, me boy!" and followed me to the office.

"You get the chair to the boss's right," I told him. "Drink?"

"Two fingers of Irish whiskey, Lad. Neat. Where might everyone be?"

"You're the first one. Hobbes won't come in till the gang's all here, especially Murphy."

"*Lieutenant* Murphy? Now, there's a rub. Make that four fingers, me friend, and tell me why he comes."

I turned my palms up. "Representative of the law, I suppose. He doesn't like you much either."

"I made him look foolish one time." Green didn't elaborate, but he was thoughtful for a minute. "Hobbes has plans for him, I'll wager."

The doorbell rang again. Marilyn and Cassius came in together; I seated them on the gray sofa with Marilyn closest to Green. When I asked about beverages, Cassius said anything cold, so long as it was non-alcoholic, and she said whatever Dad was having.

At ten minutes of two, Avery, Gloria, and Judith arrived and I put them — in that order — on the other sofa. They all refused drinks and sat silently, although Judith sent her patented icicle stare my way. Gloria seemed lost in a private world behind a rose colored veil. Avery looked exhausted, tense as a second hand jerking its way through time. He kept unfastening and fastening the flap on his briefcase. The cadence was similar to the rhythm of arthritic fingers slipping along rosary beads, and I wondered if he was praying. It was almost enough to make me feel sorry for him.

At ten minutes past two, Murphy showed up. "Damn one-way streets." He glared at me as if they were my fault, and then glared at Green before taking the chair between the two sofas.

I pulled the cord that rang the kitchen bell, although Hobbes would have known we were ready via the intercom. It was part of the Hobbes' show.

The detective wheeled in and circled around to the back of his desk. He waited while I took the chair to his left. He took a few minutes to study the former clients and Cassius, who had never been a client, but had been under suspicion, making eye contact with each of them. Satisfied, he leaned back in his wheelchair and laced his fingers together.

"One of you four," he began, "is a murderer. Twice a murderer. Almost three times a murderer. I inform you now that I know exactly who you are and —"

"Just a minute!" Murphy stood up, his bearish height and breadth towering over everyone. "Murder is police business. If you have evidence, you'd better give it to me and give it to me *now!*"

"Please, Lieutenant," Hobbes said softly. "I have asked you here because I will soon have need of you. You have expert knowledge in the newer methods of criminal identification, and later this afternoon, if you permit me to do so, I intend to tap that wealth of knowledge. Then, at the end of this meeting, after I have identified the killer of Gladys Jones, I will turn the entire murder case over to you, conclusions and evidence included. You may do with it as you will. Obviously, I need your indulgence and your help."

"Oh," Murphy said. "Oh, sure. Right. Whenever you're ready." He sat back down. I tried to catch Green's eye, to wink at him, but he was looking stone-faced at something on the ceiling.

"Unfortunately," Hobbes began again, addressing the group. "Although I believe proof exists that will convict the killer, I do not yet have it. I believe it lies below this room, but if not, it may take weeks or months of diligent searching to find it.

"Now, for one moment I speak to the murderer alone. I know you. By the end of this meeting, so will everyone else in this room, including the police and the press. It will soon be public knowledge. You do not want this. For the same reasons that you killed Gladys, you do not want this. And I do not wish to expend my resources in a prolonged and expensive inquiry.

"So I give you this opportunity to maintain your dignity and pride. If you wish to speak, do so now. You will find a simple confession to murder to be less damning than the opening of sores more than sixty years old. As you hesitate, remember this. Once I remove the cover to your box of secrets, I cannot replace it. Nor would I, if I could."

He pushed himself back from the desk. "I'll give you sixty seconds."

The room became very quiet. The clock on the mantel ticked. I tried to read the faces of those gathered. Cassius removed his glasses and began cleaning them. Gloria raised her veil for a moment and gazed at Hobbes, then lowered it. Judith looked at Gloria, then at Avery, and finally at Forrest Green. Avery noticed his hands working on his briefcase and suddenly looked around, perhaps to see if anyone was watching. No one said anything.

"Very well," Hobbes said. "We'll do it the hard way.

"Some things I know for certain, others are surmises and need confirmation, which I shall elicit from the three who originally hired me. I shall begin with a simple question. Gloria, what is the source of the tapping you say comes from Eldred?"

"It is Eldred," she said easily. "He channels the sounds across the void."

"Perhaps you believe that," Hobbes acknowledged. "And perhaps you aren't aware of how you've done it for an incredible forty years. You say you are unaware of everything because you were not yourself at the time. That is your explanation. I have a different one. Have you heard of a spiritualist by the name of Katie Fox?"

It was hard to discern if Gloria had a reaction to the name, her face hidden behind the veil, but I thought I noticed Judith go a bit pale as Hobbes continued. "More than a century ago, Katie claimed to be a channel for the spirit of a murdered man. He communicated, she said, by making tapping noises. Does that sound familiar, Miss Borden? Eventually, it was learned that she made the noises herself, by popping the knuckles in her big toes. Abel and I noticed that you held your séances barefoot. It was a convenient way to create tapping sounds when you needed them, wasn't it?"

She remained unperturbed. "It's what Eldred does."

"When you hired me, you talked about solving an 'old, old mystery.' Now is the time to tell me what that mystery is."

Gloria removed her veil and held it in her lap. She answered slowly. "Why did Eldred choose me? Why does he never leave me alone?"

"No, Miss Borden. You know the answers to those questions. They aren't the mystery. Perhaps what you want to know is why he left you."

She said sharply, "He never left me!"

Avery interrupted. "Let her be. Please."

Hobbes turned his head a fraction and studied the trembling lawyer. "Do you know what happened to Eldred, Mr. Regasmun?"

Avery shook his head. "You're doing the talking."

"All right. Let me tell you some of the things I do know. Gloria's and Judith's last name is not Borden. They were born into an historic and noble family, whose name was 'Albany,'" He grimaced. "They were born in this very house and lived here for thirty-five years. Then something happened, so they moved to Chicago and changed their name.

"The first time the three of you came here, I thought you were shocked by the antics of Sally. I was wrong. It was by the sudden realization that you were in *this* house, the ancestral house you took such pains to escape."

I watched their expressions as Hobbes was talking, but aside from Cassius slowly putting on his glasses, none of the four moved. I did see Forrest Green on the other side of the desk, writing in his notebook. Marilyn, alone, looked surprised by the revelation.

"In nineteen-twenty," Hobbes continued, "two years before the Albany girls were born, another set of twins had been delivered. Boys, to a Mr. and Mrs.

Stone. The sons were named Avery and Eldred. They, too, were raised in Meridian in a house by the river.

"So, to whom am I talking? Two Bordens and a Regasmun, or two Albanys and a Stone?"

"Three Albanys, you mean," Murphy interjected.

"A good observation, Lieutenant. But for the moment, I wish to exclude the younger Cassius.

"Now, do any of you have anything to say? By which names should I call you?"

"Our legal names are Borden and Regasmun," Avery answered.

Hobbes nodded. "So it shall be. For today, and to avoid confusion, I will call you Gloria, Judith, and Avery.

"The four of you spent your childhood just blocks from each other. Two of you became close friends. Closer than friends. Eldred, as people said then, had put Gloria in the family way. To avoid a public scandal, she and her mother moved to Galena, where they stayed until the baby was born. When they returned, her mother claimed Cassius was hers, and raised him as a son."

"Wait, wait, wait!" Marilyn stood up. "That would mean Aunt Gloria is my grandmother!"

Cassius took her hand and gently pulled her back down. "And my mother," he added.

"You knew?"

"Since I was a boy, when I wondered why my eyes were brown while my sisters' eyes were blue, and

259

how a woman almost fifty years old could have a baby. Some friend pointed out the obvious and told me the rumor he'd heard." He patted her hand. "It could be a lot worse."

"Did you ever talk to Gloria and Eldred about it?" Hobbes asked Cassius.

"To Eldred once, when I was nineteen. He laughed and said I'd been lucky. That a lot of babies made that way never got born. I wanted to kill him."

"Did you?"

"He disappeared. What do you think?"

"Would you have also killed Gladys?"

"We're a strange family, Car'l, but I would not have harmed Gladys."

Nevertheless, Murphy hitched his chair closer to the gray sofa and rested his ham-like hand on Cassius shoulder.

"At our first meeting, your sisters, excuse me, your mother and aunt and Avery, hired me — explaining that you sought control of their fortune. I do not believe that to be true. Was it?"

"No. Avery was the one who had too much control. I didn't trust him. I wanted him away from my... from Gloria and Judith."

"Anger, vengeance, distrust. They all make good motives," Hobbes said. "But sometimes, there are better ones." He turned his attention to the sister who was younger by eighteen minutes, but now looked older by eighteen years.

Stephen Stillwell

"You once said that men are fickle, Judith, because of Eldred's sudden disappearance. You were very bitter about it. Were you also in love with him?"

"What if I was, Mr. Hobbes? He was a talented man, a charming man. He was an artist. Many women admired him." Avery groaned softly, and turned his head to the wall. She continued, "You wonder if I could have killed Eldred out of jealousy? Never." She looked at Avery in disgust. "Him, easily."

"Why him?"

"He's a lawyer. No. Lawyers are honorable. Avery's a shyster. He had contacts with the Chicago mob. Eldred was gentle — Avery was an opportunist. He appeared early in the summer of Eldred's disappearance and made a play for Gloria. He would have brought shame to our family!" Her voice had risen and become shrill.

"Yet he has been with you for forty years."

"Gloria required him. We needed someone to manage our finances, and he has done that well," she admitted grudgingly, her voice returning to normal.

"Two more motives," Hobbes murmured. "Jealousy and pride. Are there others?

"Mr. Regasmun," he said sharply. "Are there others?"

"How would I know?"

"Where does the money come from?"

"Money?"

"To run the house on Belleview. Mr. Green has had the Bordens' finances investigated. Their

261

inheritance has long since been exhausted; the revenue from the séances is meager, regardless of what has been said. Yet they live well. A multi-million dollar house, a Mercedes... Where does the money come from?"

"Green is mistaken. There is adequate money."

"Do you make a lot of money, Avery?"

"Enough."

"Enough to agree to my fee without hesitation? A very large fee? Do you make much, much more than that? Do you make ten million dollars a year?"

Avery didn't answer.

"Have you heard of the Triton Corporation?"

The lawyer still didn't respond.

"Lieutenant Murphy has heard of it."

The officer decided he had and said, "Damn right."

Hobbes continued, "Its logo along with its name, were on your computer's monitor the night Abel found Gladys' body; seeing it almost cost him his life.

"Ironically, the logo for Triton meant nothing by itself; if it hadn't been for the warning shots, Abel would have had no reason to remember seeing it. But, the shots had the effect of fixing everything he had seen in and around the Borden's house in his subconscious. Even so, your relations with Triton might never have been found out, except for the quirkiness of fate." He studied Regasmun for a moment, but the lawyer seemed unmoved.

"Fate provided help from a quite unexpected source." He stroked the ends of his long droopy moustache in homage to fate, which might have been the only supernatural force he believed in. Not that he'd ever admit it. "And I'm sure the help was unintended.

"It came from Katya Ransom when she and Abel crossed paths and Katya made some unpleasant remarks to Abel. She said, among other things, that he should have become an astronaut and crashed on one of the planet Neptune's moons.

Chapter 30

"Triton is one of those moons, but, according to Mr. Green, Triton is also a corporation that deals in counterfeit money. That is the connection you feared Abel would make. You, Triton, and counterfeiting.

Hobbes took a deep breath and continued, "So, the gunshots, Katya's comment about the moon of Neptune, and the attempt on his life, all together, they suddenly made sense. You were simply covering up your connection to Triton.

"So again I ask, do you make ten million a year? Are you a counterfeiter?"

Avery shook his head. "I would have had no talent for that. Eldred was the artist, not me."

"So he was." Hobbes pulled at the ends of his moustache. He put his hands on the wheel rails and slowly rolled around the desk. He stopped a yard away from Avery. They studied each other, eye to eye, then Hobbes said slowly and carefully, "And he still is an artist, isn't he? After all, it wasn't Eldred who was killed, was it? The murdered man was Avery. And it is Avery who has lain, hidden behind bricks and mortar, in the basement of this house for almost half a century.

"Eldred, the artist who could make counterfeit money and copy Monet, but had no skill at laying bricks, still lives. Yes, Eldred Stone lives."

The lawyer seemed to shrink into himself. "You have to be so damn smart," he whispered.

"You had no talent for practicing law. So you had to leave Meridian and go somewhere where you could pretend to be a lawyer."

Eldred, formerly Avery, was silent.

"My guess is you disappeared for a while, and, through contacts with *Triton,* learned the business of printing and passing your own money. You opened a law office in Chicago, persuaded Judith and Gloria to buy the house on Belleview, and became their attorney." Hobbes drummed his fingers on the desk. "You are a man of many talents, Mr. Stone."

The office was silent for a moment, then Gloria looked closely at the man she had known as Avery.

"Eldred? Eldred?" She said in her strange quiet way. She seemed to see him for the first time. "Can it really be you?" She touched his hand softly. "Are you really Eldred?"

I had to give the old girl credit. She was accepting this reality quicker than anyone else.

Hobbes raised his hand and his voice. "Eldred Stone. Yes, I present Eldred Stone." He looked at the man again. "What should I call you?"

"I've been Avery for forty years. I'm tired of it. It would be pleasant to be Eldred again."

"Then Eldred it will be."

Eldred sighed. "How did you know?"

"The '*Eldred*' on the counterfeit bills. I suppose it was one of the few ways that you could put your name to your art. It was apparent, too, that you had to be alive to keep the engravings up to date. Then, there were the bricks you put up around Abel. Uneven and sloppy. When your brother was young, he had developed a formidable skill as a bricklayer, yet neither wall of the tombs erected in my basement indicated any level of skill. Finally, you gave up the law practice in *Meridian*. Why? Because you had to. You are not a lawyer. And then you admitted to loving Gloria before Cassius was born, implying you were his father.

"But why murder your brother? And why kill Gladys?"

Gloria interrupted, her words sounding distant, sad. "Why didn't you tell me? All those years..."

Eldred ignored her. "I am not a killer."

Hobbes said, "You have old scars on your face that weren't in the pictures." When Eldred looked surprised Hobbes continued, "Yes, we have copies of the pictures Gladys died for. They were interred with the corpse of your brother. I believe the coroner will find bits of skin under the dead man's fingernails. I believe they came from your face.

"Lieutenant Murphy, in your expert opinion, is it possible that forty year old human skin can have retained enough of its identity to be used as evidence?"

Murphy hadn't known about the body in the basement before now, and he may have known nothing about genetic matching, but he was an expert at sounding like an expert. He was used to inventing facts, and he knew what Hobbes wanted.

"Body sealed in an airtight room for forty years? They've had success with three-thousand year old mummies."

"Then the proof is there. The question is why? What was the motive?

"Was it jealousy? Your brother was making a play for Gloria. Did you kill him with an ax? Entomb him in the basement? But why switch identities? Did Gloria see the murder, but not the murderer, and think it was Eldred who had been killed? Did you become Avery to stay close to Gloria?"

Hobbes made a face. "That's a lot of questions. Most of them are irrelevant. There are some far more important. They come back to Gladys and what she said to Abel, 'She ain't going to jail, is she?' and, 'she was in love, and he weren't.' Gladys was talking about a woman, someone guilty of a terrible crime. Who was that woman? What was the crime? And why were the pictures important?"

The only response I could see was from Judith. She dropped her gaze and stared at the floor. *She knows,* I thought.

"The pictures were suggestive," he said. "One brother holding an ax over the head of the other. They would divert suspicion from the real killer, perhaps, but they also told the nature of the crime. Murder by ax. Who was the woman? That can be answered by another question.

"There is an old English children's rhyme that speaks of similar murders:

'Lizzie Borden took an ax,

Gave her mother forty whacks.'

"The man in the basement below us was killed with a hatchet, a small ax if you will, so the words are suggestive. Changing the family name from Albany to Borden has significance only when you know both the rhyme and the nature of the killing.

"The question is, who chose the name, 'Borden?' I think only the murderer would see the irony of the name. Only the person who insisted I come to a séance so that Eldred could talk to me."

Gloria nodded. "Eldred chose the name, and Eldred insisted you come."

"And I talked to him, didn't I? In that brief conversation, Eldred, speaking through you, told me that Gladys was 'sitting and waiting and died.'"

"She stopped with him for a while on her way through."

Hobbes took a deep breath. "So it would seem. That could explain how he knew the nature of her death."

"Just a minute," Murphy interrupted. "Just a damn minute. You're talking like you believe that crap!"

Hobbes raised a hand, "That's a good observation, Lieutenant. I was in fact talking to Eldred, or at least to that part of Gloria that she had given to him. The important thing was that, speaking through Gloria, he had told me how Gladys had died. And he told me long before her body was found. Those were details only the murderer would have known." Hobbes had begun speaking directly to Gloria; the rest of us were simply bystanders. "Of course it wasn't Eldred talking. There never was an Eldred talking. Guilt was the speaker. You wanted to be found out, Gloria, but not consciously. That was no paranormal revelation. Eldred wasn't revealing any supernatural secret. It was the killer making a confession."

He fell silent, waiting for a response. We all waited, all but one of us. Finally, Gloria spoke, softly, abstractly. "I understand now. That was so many years ago. I thought he was Eldred. I thought the man I killed was Eldred. He had abandoned me twenty years before, and he had come back, and I thought I was losing him again. I had seen him with that other woman, and followed him here, where we had met many times. I could not bear to share him. He had gone too far. I had to put a stop to his cheating. I said we could look at some pictures of us that Gladys had taken, and we entered the basement. A hatchet had been left out, and it lay on the bench. When he turned his back to look at the pictures, I picked it up and used it.

"Afterwards, as he lay dying, I knew I had acted foolishly. I had killed my only love. But it was too late." Her face reflected the sadness of forty years lost. Then, as if she was suddenly aware of new hope, she looked up at Eldred/Avery's face, seeing Eldred. "I chose the name, of course." She sounded enchanted. "Who else?"

"Who else," Hobbes repeated. "Because of Eldred you had a baby. Because of him, you had to give up the right to be the child's mother. Instead you spent years watching Cassius grow up in the same house, raised as the son of another woman.

"You bore that all, alone, for twenty years, and then he returned. He romanced you. You fell in love again. Later, you learned of the dalliance with Ellie Fox, not knowing it was really Avery who had dallied. Did you plan revenge before the night of the killing, or did it just happen, as you said? Did you bring the man you thought was Eldred to this house knowing the ax was still there?"

Eldred cried out. "Enough! Enough. It was my fault, not hers. I shirked responsibility when Cassius was born. And for twenty years, I was a vagabond, a scoundrel, and finally an artist. When I returned to Meridian, I found that Gloria had become even more beautiful and irresistible. But again I wasn't ready for a real commitment, and because of that Avery began impersonating me. First, there was a schoolteacher; I didn't remember her name at first ..."

"Ellen Fox," Gloria murmured.

"Ellen Fox. That's right. It wasn't much of a secret that in my youth I had an affair with Ellen, but I broke it off. I decided I wanted only Gloria. But then Avery pretended to be me and made up with Ellen. He had pretended to be me many times before, and I really never minded, but this time Gloria saw them. That same night, he went too far. He tried to take my place with Gloria, and it cost him his life."

Hobbes studied him for a long moment. "And then you became her cleanup man?"

Eldred nodded. "She found me that night, called me Avery, and took me to where my brother was. He died in my arms. In his final struggle to live, he scratched my face. I carried him into the basement and laid him under the stairs, and exchanged billfolds. I gave him the pictures to keep him company during the long darkness. It was late at night; no one at the brickyard saw me load bricks and mortar onto the truck. You know the rest."

"The counterfeiting you did to support the household."

The man nodded.

"And Gladys?"

"I swear I knew nothing of her danger. I wouldn't have let it happen." His voice broke, and tears wet his eyes. He tried to choke back a sob. It was a sound I'd heard before. "Gloria knew Gladys had some pictures. She had known it for years. I think Gloria came to believe that one of them showed her killing Eldred. Guilt and fear of people finding her out made her into a murderer, again. She wasn't really responsible, you know. She hasn't been for forty years."

He looked toward the window as if he needed to gather his thoughts. "I shouldn't have let this investigation begin at all. There was no need for it, and now Gladys is dead."

Eldred opened and closed his briefcase without even glancing in. Then, he shifted in his chair, obviously a bit restless and nervous.

"And what about Abel?" Hobbes asked.

Eldred looked at me as if I'd asked the question, not Hobbes. "Ah, yes, what about you, Abel?" He spoke slowly and apologetically.

"Part of Gloria wanted the truth found out. The Eldred part. And she didn't want anyone else hurt, so I tried to warn you. I had those shots fired, but you ignored them.

"The other part of her would do anything to keep it a secret. Saturday night, she had me drive

271

down here so, she said, she could plead with you. We waited in the car until you and Marilyn returned to the boathouse, then she went by herself to talk to you.

Gloria said she would wait in the basement with the light on. I should have known what she had in mind, and I could have stopped her. It was only till later that I realized how much of a fool I'd been. Half an hour after Marilyn left, Gloria came back and collapsed in the car, exhausted. She said she had killed you, and dragged you under the stairs."

The rhythmic opening and closing of his briefcase started again. "I'm truly sorry, Mr. Houston. I thought you were dead. When the boy came down the stairs, I hid, thinking I'd finish after he was gone. Then, we heard you moan. He ran for help and I left. I am grateful you are alive."

"Yeah," I said. "So am I."

He slumped down and took a deep breath as if preparing to say more, but Hobbes spoke first.

"I have two questions that have puzzled me since the beginning," he said. "Who suggested coming to me, and why?"

"I did, Mr. Hobbes," Gloria answered. "I didn't want to, but a voice from the other side demanded that I do so. It... He wanted justice served. He wanted... closure."

"Not Eldred?" Hobbes asked.

"Eldred was a name I gave him." She smiled suddenly, lighting up the room. "I suppose it could have been the real Avery."

"And has justice been served?"

272

"It soon will be." The false Avery's voice was suddenly quiet, calm. It sounded at peace. He stood up and helped Gloria to her feet, then slipped his hand into his briefcase and pulled out a small revolver.

"I beg you all to stay here," he said. "It's time I told my brother 'goodbye.'"

"No, my darling Eldred," Gloria said softly, and brought the hand holding the gun gently to her lips. "It's time we told him 'hello.'"

They backed to the door. "We know the way," he said.

Murphy started to follow them, but Hobbes blocked the door with his wheelchair. "Let it be," he said.

A few moments later, we heard the first shot, and then a moment later, the second.

Murphy growled, and Hobbes moved out of the way. The homicide detective headed for the basement.

After a time, Judith began to cry.

Epilogue

Two weeks later, Forrest Green, Hobbes, and I sat in the office testing cheap beers and talking about the case.

"Where did they get the name 'Carpunky?'" I asked.

Green's face turned a little red. "You might have blamed the *Echo* for that, Laddie. About that time, there was a tragic song, a very popular song, about a punk; a boy, self-centered and full of pity and loathing for himself, was killed in a car race. The managing editor thought it would be clever to use the song to make a name, so he took 'car' and 'punk,' which was how he pictured the boy, and made 'Carpunky.'

"Is that a fact?" I said. Green ignored my skepticism and turned to the boss.

"A stroke of genius it was, Car'l, me good fellow, to bring the lieutenant Murphy in for the final meeting." He took a drink, made a face, and set the nearly full bottle in the discard box.

Hobbes acknowledged the compliment with a nod. "It was a necessity. I had waited a day to call the police about finding the body, and my license could have been in jeopardy. He has a way of getting those minor details ignored."

"Only way to get rid of 'im." He set another bottle in the reject box. "Where'd you get this poison?"

"From the refrigerator," I answered. "But before we get into that, I need to ask a question about something that has really begun to bother me."

"Of course," said Hobbes.

"Ask away, me boy," said Green.

"What happened to Wilder and Ravenkill? I've been thinking a little about them, and as near as I can tell, they haven't been seen since that night... that night that I..."

It was still hard to talk about how I had tried to kill Hobbes, but parts of that night still bothered me, "I know it's over, but I still need to know what has happened to them."

"They be unlikely to bother you again, me boy."

"The police didn't even look for them, did they? Where did they go? Mexico, South America? What about the witches?"

"Should I tell the boy, Car'l or would you rather?"

"Tell him what you found at the *Echo,* and I'll tell him the rest."

"And gladly I'll do it," the little green man said. "A night or two after they disappeared, I went to Wilder's office, by meself, and found the authentic and complete Borden files. I looked them over and, me boy, I understood everything about the Bordens and what Wilder had planned for them.

"What got Mr. Wilder started was Sally's trip to that newspaper, and her simple request to look at the Bordens' file. Mr. Wilder refused her, of course, but then he went and looked at the file for himself, seeing as how Car'l Hobbes was interested in it. Everything was there.

All the research that you five did had been done before. A gifted reporter, that man of forty years ago had been, but he foolishly approached the Bordens about his findings. Then, he simply disappeared.

"Wilder saw a double opportunity staring him in the face. He could use Car'l's need for a look at those files as a way to get vengeance for the shame and embarrassment he had suffered at his hand, and he could get a fortune in blackmail from the Bordens.

"He also knew of Ravenkill's hatred for you, me boy, and she was eager to be a part of Wilder's masterful plan. It took wings of its own. They could use you to kill Hobbes, and the revenge would be doubly sweet.

"Me man Hobbes saw through the mischief in time and removed the bullets from your pistol. You know the rest of that part of the story. Now Car'l will tell you what happened to our friends Tom and Pamela."

Hobbes drew his fingers down to the edges of his moustache, "Think for a minute about Judith Borden and what she said the day they disappeared. She was sitting in that chair," he pointed to one of the straight backs.

"First, she said, 'That vile reporter, Thomas Wilder, from the *National Echo,* and his equally vile girlfriend came to our house Thursday morning'. Next she said, 'Gloria took pleasure in their company as she does with all fools and innocents, and persuaded me to go to my room and allow her to handle them.'"

That was enough of an explanation. I could guess the rest.

"Fools and innocents," I repeated. "They didn't know what they were getting into, did they. One old woman...." I let it fade away.

She would have found it simple enough to lure them down the stairs and into the basement. Maybe just saying that is where they keep the money would have been enough to get a greedy overconfident blackmailer and his girlfriend to follow her.

Disposing of the bodies wouldn't have been hard. Avery would have helped. What were two more killings?

I had only one more comment and a question. "Buried in their basement, I suppose. Will you call the police?"

"Probably not," he said. "What would be the point? The guilty have been punished, and justice has been served."

My spirits were lifted. The world would not be worse off without Pamela Ravenkill and Tom Wilder.

Then, things got even better.

The doorbell rang. "I'll get it," I said. I was expecting a visitor.

It wasn't who I was looking for. Instead, it was a deliveryman. For Mr. Hobbes, he said. He unloaded three cases of beer, every bottle different, on the floor by the desk.

There was a letter with the beer. Hobbes read it and passed it to Green without comment. Forrest read it twice, and then gave it to me.

"Hobbes," it said, "I appreciate your help in solving the Gladys Jones case. I may get a promotion from it. They've asked me to be your liaison anytime you need help from the Chicago police, or they need help from you. I saw your book. None of these beers is listed in it."

It was signed, "Murph."

We looked at each other for a long moment. The doorbell rang again.

Green finally broke the silence. "Well, now, and suppose you tell me what the apostrophe is for, Car'l?"

I didn't hear the answer as I went to the door again.

"Care for a boat ride, Mr. Paranormal Snoop?" the visitor asked.

About The Author

Diagnosed with Parkinson's disease in 1994, Steve Stillwell retired from his work as a master electrician the following year. This allowed him to pursue his lifelong dream of becoming a writer. He returned to college and took several creative writing classes. Since then, he has written three novels and more than one hundred poems and short stories.

Steve and his wife live in Bourbonnais, Illinois.